I WAS NOT IN THE MOOD TO BE TEASED.

"So—so how come you changed the rules?" I stuttered. "How come now it's about going to Earth all on your own, and baby-sitting some human stranger single-handed? Not to mention, ooh, protecting them from the Powers of Darkness! Frankly I don't think anyone in this hall is ready for that much responsibility." My voice was squeaky with fear.

LOOK FOR THESE OTHER TITLES IN THE

ANGELS UNLIMITED SERIES:

1 **Winging It**

2 **Losing the Plot**

3 **Flying High**

ANGELS UNLIMITED 4

Calling the Shots

Annie Dalton

AVON BOOKS
An Imprint of Harper Collins*Publishers*

To Maria with love and thanks

for invaluable help

For information address HarperCollins Children's Books, a division of HarperCollins Publishers, 1350 Avenue of the Americas, New York, NY 10019.
First published in Great Britain in 2002 by Collins, an imprint of HarperCollins Publishers Ltd., 77-85 Fulham Palace Road, Hammersmith, London W6 8JB.

Library of Congress Catalog Card Number: 2002093377
ISBN 0-06-008818-4

First Avon edition, 2003

❖

Visit us on the World Wide Web!
www.harperchildrens.com

Chapter One

WHEN I WAS ALIVE, I had totally the wrong idea about Heaven.

Each time I heard the word, this spooky film footage came up on my mental screen. I'd picture myself wandering ankle-deep in little fluffy clouds through a vast empty waiting room. Apart from the heavenly Muzak playing over the PA system, there wasn't a sound. No swoosh of traffic, no pounding hip-hop beat, no chatting, laughing or crying. *Nada*. Omigosh, I'd think, if this is Heaven, what must that other place be like!

Then, twenty-four hours after my thirteenth birthday, I was knocked down by some youth in a speeding car and *bam*! I was checking out the heavenly facilities for real.

Not only that, I had been talent-spotted to be a trainee angel! I have no idea how that happened and I don't really care. The good news is you can all relax. There *is* no cloud-filled waiting room.

I live bang in the middle of a big, buzzy, beautiful city, filled with shops, cafés and the loveliest gardens you ever saw. The beach is like, minutes away. Lola and I go there constantly.

It's weird to think that if I hadn't died, Lola and I would never have met, because originally she's from the twenty-second century. Her full name is Lola Sanchez, also known as Lollie. We met on my first day here and I'm not exaggerating, we are total soul mates. We love the same fashions, the exact same music, and are both deeply dedicated shoppers.

I've shocked you, haven't I? You had *no* idea it was possible to go shopping in Heaven! But like Lola says, "Well, duh! Who do you think invented shopping malls in the first place!"

Don't go thinking my new life is one long heavenly beach party. I still go to school, remember. The sole purpose of the Academy is to train us to be celestial agents; angels in other words. This means the Agency (that's like, Angel HQ) is constantly monitoring our progress. Plus my teacher, Mr. Allbright, doesn't let us get away with a thing. I have never studied so hard in my whole existence as I do in that guy's class.

To be honest, I never saw the point of school when I was alive. My teachers made everything *so* boring. Even history, if you can believe that. The Angel Academy takes a much more hands-on approach. We don't just memorize dates and read books. We genuinely experience history.

Yes, I'm talking actual time-travel! This is not mere time tourism, okay? We're training to be celestial trouble-shooters, so we have to do everything the professional agents do. Lola and I are now so hooked that we signed up to study Earth history as our special subject. It's like I finally found what I was created for.

And yet . . . I still didn't totally believe I was an angel.

Oh, I *looked* the part! When I checked in the mirror there I was, glowing with that rosy angel glow, in my favorite school casuals with the cool Academy logo. I had my new ID in my wallet. I had my official angel name (it's Helix). Plus I already had several angelic missions safely under my belt.

But somewhere inside I still thought of myself as the same old Melanie Beeby, the insecure girl I used to be, before that joyrider booted me out of the twenty-first century into the Afterlife.

Then something happened which completely changed my attitude.

Lola and I were in our favorite department store on an urgent mission to buy her the ultimate pair of biker boots. We sailed up the escalator, yakking away, when with absolutely no warning, the entire store started rushing away from me; sort of like a tidal wave in reverse.

In the blink of an eye, all the shoppers, bright lights, and displays of cute celestial handbags were miles below, looking exactly like a pretty pattern in a kid's kaleidoscope.

My actual body was still traveling up the escalator. I could feel my fingers clinging on to the handrail. But my inner angel or whatever stared down with interest from its new perch in outer space.

Snatches of conversation zipped past. There was a gale of girly laughter, so close it tickled. Someone was plonking out a tune on an old-fashioned piano and someone else started singing, "Put another nickel in, in the nickelodeon." And the whole time, I could feel this unknown force pulling and tugging at me.

Then like a cosmic rubber band, I pinged back

to the department store. I staggered off the escalator, totally weirded out.

"Boo, are you okay?" Lola was asking anxiously. I don't know why she calls me Boo. Lola is constantly giving her mates weird nicknames.

"I'm great," I gulped. "We'll find you those biker boots if it's the last thing we do!"

Lola shook her head. "Change of plan, babe."

She steered me firmly toward the down escalator. Minutes later we were sitting at one of Guru's outdoor tables in the sun. Mo brought our smoothies, waving away my ID. "It's on the house," he insisted. "You look like you need them. I bet you skipped breakfast, am I right?"

I gave him a feeble grin. "Yeah yeah, it's the most important meal of the day."

"You said it," called Mo and he disappeared into the kitchen.

Guru's strawberry smoothies are really something else. After a couple of sips I felt new strength flowing through my veins.

"That's better," said Lola. "You had me worried, Boo. You went white."

"Don't be such an old lady," I growled. "It's like Mo said. I had low blood sugar or something."

As a trainee angel, I'm constantly exposed to paranormal events when I'm on duty. But when I get home, I expect life to putter along in a happy heavenly groove. The idea that an unknown force could like, *toy* with me any time it fancied, totally confused me.

Two days later it happened again.

We were having a class martial arts session. Lola and I were in a three with our buddy, Reuben. Mr. Allbright had just shown us this cool move called the Waterfall. To get it right, you have to unplug your mind and become pure angelic energy, something I'd always found impossible. But this time I was a bit too successful, because three, four, five times, I went whirling through the air, chanting, "I am pure angelic energy. I am pure angelic energy . . ." Then—*whoosh*! I completely left my body.

Once again I was floating past stars and planets, to the tinny soundtrack of that bizarre nickelodeon song.

Then Reuben and I banged heads and all three of us fell in a heap.

Lola rubbed her nose. "Ow! What happened?"

"I think that was me," I said. "I kind of lost my concentration."

Lola and Reuben exchanged meaningful looks. "Then she must be punished," said Reuben gleefully.

Squealing with laughter, I joined in their play fight, until Mr. Allbright made us break it up.

I know, I know, I should have told my mates. But I couldn't somehow. Once I said the words out loud, I'd be admitting my terrifying experiences were real.

That night I was afraid to go to bed in case the mysterious force snatched me out of Heaven the minute I fell asleep. Once I dozed off in my chair and I literally felt myself rising out of my seat, but I got a grip just in time. And that creepy nickelodeon song was going round and round my head until I thought I'd go nuts.

Finally I did what I always do when I'm having a disturbed night. I stuck my headphones on and listened to the special CD that Reuben had burned for me.

Unlike Lollie and me, Reuben is pure angel. He's not like, a saint or anything. He's actually a bit of a party animal. When we first hooked up, Lola and I played him all our favorite Earth tunes and he went into this major rapture! After that, he refused to give us a moment's peace until we agreed to give him DJ lessons.

But like Lola says, our work is totally done! Our buddy turned out to be a natural angel DJ. We've actually adopted one of his mixes as our theme song. There's a bit that goes, "You're not alone. You're not alone." And I swear it has healing powers, because I played it over and over until the sky was growing light outside my window, and suddenly the lyrics genuinely got through to me.

I'm *not* alone, I thought. We're the three cosmic musketeers, like Lola says. There's nothing I can't tell those guys.

I decided it was now officially morning. I showered, dressed, and went to knock on Lola's door. She came to the door in her PJs, looking unbelievably frazzled.

"Get moving, sleepyhead," I teased. "If we hurry, we can grab breakfast at Guru, on the way to school."

My soul mate was in a strangely crabby mood. "Honestly, Mel, can't you do anything by yourself?" she snapped.

"Hey, I offered to buy you breakfast," I said huffily. "No need to bite my head off."

"Sorry, babe," she mumbled. "Just had a bad

night. Later, yeah?" She closed the door, leaving me in the corridor.

I felt like crying. I had no idea why my best friend was being so mean.

Then things got worse. When I got to school, Reuben, normally the sweetest boy in the universe, practically blanked me! And Lola made it offensively obvious that she wasn't interested in anything I had to say. For some reason my mates had completely gone off me. I must have done something terrible without realizing.

Unfortunately I had no chance to find out what, because Mr. Allbright kept us slaving away all morning. My problem would have to keep until the evening. It was Wednesday, and on Wednesday afternoons angel trainees go off to do their own thing: talk to trees, go scuba diving or whatever.

Chase, one of Reuben's weirder buddies, hangs out with the tigers in a wildlife park. Reuben spends his private study time improving his martial arts. And every Wednesday my soul mate goes down to the beach where she sings her heart out to the wind and the waves. Lollie has a brilliant singing voice.

I used to get *so* depressed on Wednesdays. It

seemed as if everyone but me had some special talent. Also I *hate* being by myself. I sometimes get really scared when I'm on my own, as if I'm actually going to dissolve or disappear or something.

Then one day some little nursery-school kids found me on the seashore and took me back to school. And I discovered that I do have a talent—for hanging out with preschool angels! I go there most weeks now to help out Miss Dove with her class.

This particular afternoon we were making a class collage of my old solar system. Everyone got stuck in, using scrumpled tissue paper, masses of shiny gold and silver stars, and about a ton of glitter.

Then for the third and final time, my heavenly surroundings dropped away. *This* time all my resistance had gone. This time I longed to go where the mysterious force wanted to take me. This time the force and I were like, *one*.

I floated through the glittering void in total awe. I swooshed through pearly swirls of newborn galaxies, past silent planets crusted with ice, and hot hyperactive planets spewing out rainbow-colored gases. Finally I saw Earth far below, with its shimmery blue oceans and jewel-green forests. And then across time and space, I heard someone calling to me.

"Who are you?" I whispered. "What do you want?"

Then the cosmic elastic twanged me back to the classroom. I think I'd fainted at some point, because Miss Dove had pushed my head down between my knees and all the little angels were gazing at me with fascinated expressions. Omigosh, I'm really ill, I panicked. I've caught some rare cosmic disease that no one ever talks about.

But Miss Dove just beamed down at me, as if my weird fainting spell was like, an Oscar-winning achievement. "It is disturbing the first time you get the Call," she said calmly. "But you get used to it."

"The Call?" I quavered.

She gave me a warm smile. "You'd better run along. The Agency will want to brief you before you leave."

I seemed to have turned into her echo. "Leave?" I repeated in bewilderment. "Where am I going?"

"Tell her, someone!" said Miss Dove.

A little boy stepped forward. "Someone on Earth needs a guardian angel, Melanie," he said shyly. "And there's absolutely *no* time to lose."

Chapter Two

I HAD BEEN AT THE Angel Academy over three terms now. If I had to, I could find my way around blindfolded. I was equally at home off-campus. I could tell you where to go for the ultimate breakfast (Guru, obviously), the coolest place to go dancing (the Babylon Café), and the place to find that very special outfit (the Source).

Yet I was so ignorant of the basics of angel existence, I had mistaken a natural cosmic phenomenon for like, an imaginary disease!

"You have got to finish reading that Angel Handbook, Melanie," I scolded myself, as I headed into town. "You are a total disgrace."

But I have to admit I was secretly thrilled. I have always wanted to be a guardian angel. Okay, that's not strictly true. Back on Earth, I was desperate to be rich and famous. But then I died and the rich and famous scenario seemed kind of passé, and my guardian angel fantasy gradually took over. I'd never told anyone, obviously. The training takes like, eons, and anyway, I'd look a real twit if it didn't happen. I think I might have mentioned that I was not exactly a big success at my old school? My teacher, Miss Rowntree, thought I was a complete ditz. "An airhead with attitude," she called me once.

Luckily I didn't need to worry about Miss Rowntree's opinion anymore. I started to dance along the street. "I'm an angel!" I sang out. "A real, live, bona fide angel. I got the Call. Woo! I got the Call!"

I recognized a familiar figure up ahead; a honey-colored boy in faded cut-offs. Tiny dreads whipped around his head as he hurried downtown. It's Wednesday, how come Reuben isn't doing martial arts? I thought. Then I got it!

"Hey, wait for me!" I ran to catch him up. "You got the Call, didn't you?" I panted. "That's why you were being so weird in school."

Reuben's eyes opened wide. "You mean you . . . ?"

"I thought I was going nuts!" I admitted. "I had this spooky song going round my head."

"Hey! I'm the hotshot DJ," he objected. "Why

didn't I get a song?"

"Do you think anyone else—" I began.

I heard footsteps flying along behind us. "You might have waited, you monsters!" Lola gasped.

"This is *so* sublime," I breathed. All three of us had been Called.

Lollie looked guilty. "Boo, about this morning—I'd had this weird night and I—"

"Forget it." I grinned. "Everyone stresses out the first time, Miss Dove says."

"This is happening, right? I'm not just dreaming I'm going to be a guardian angel?" Reuben was in a daze of happiness.

Lola patted his back, laughing. "It's happening, Sweetpea!"

"I can't take it in," he burbled. "I'd never even been to Earth until last term. Now I'm going solo."

My stomach totally looped the loop, and Reuben's words echoed round my brain. *Going solo, going solo . . .*

I mean, I was still honored and everything. I simply hadn't expected to be doing the full-on guardian angel thing so soon. In my guardian angel fantasies I'd been calmer, and wiser and well, *older*.

We had almost reached the Agency building. In a city of gorgeous buildings it's still a major landmark; a soaring skyscraper built from some special celestial glass which constantly changes color, almost as if it's alive. We turned the corner as the building was turning from shimmery hyacinth to a sparkling cornflower blue.

My eyes were still dazzled as I followed the others through the revolving doors. The guy at the desk waved us toward the lifts without even glancing at our ID.

"That's a first," Lola whispered.

A scary first, I thought. This is how they treat grown-up.

We made our way to the hall where we have our briefing sessions. To my surprise it was packed with angel trainees, including Amber, a girl from our class, and Reuben's mate Chase (the kid who hangs out with tigers). I'd been cogratulating myself on breaking into some cosmic elite. But apparently angel trainees were being Called constantly. I just hadn't known about it.

Amber waved and we went to sit with her and Tiger Boy.

A bunch of junior agents came in. "Michael says sorry to keep you, but he's on his way," one said apologetically.

Chase gave me a grin. "Must be having trouble with your century again, Mel."

"There are other centuries," I said huffily.

We started chatting amongst ourselves. It turned out we'd all been freaked by our first experience of the Call.

"It just seemed way too huge," Amber confessed.

"I know," I said eagerly. "You think no one else could understand."

Michael arrived at last and everyone instantly stopped talking. Michael is our headmaster, but if you're picturing an old buffer with elbow patches, forget it. He's an archangel, one of the advanced beings who keeps the cosmos running smoothly, plus he's a major player at the Agency.

From the outside, he's just a big tired guy in a crumpled suit. But as he scanned along the rows of trainees, his eyes met mine and I shivered with awe. Even in that crowded hall, Michael knew exactly where I was. If he wanted to, he could see right into my soul.

His voice was matter-of-fact. "No doubt you're all wondering why your teachers didn't warn you about your recent ordeal."

"Don't say it! 'Some things can't be explained in words,' wah wah wah," Lola called out daringly.

Michael smiled. "Precisely. They have to be experienced. For a short time each of you felt confused and alone. You couldn't understand how such a thing could occur in Heaven. You worried that you were imagining it, or what's the phrase, 'losing it'?"

"Boy did I lose it," muttered Reuben. "I could hear creaking sails and ocean waves."

"I got thundering hooves," Lola hissed. "Anyone else get that?"

"I just got a bizarre little song," I hissed back.

There was a buzz of voices as trainees eagerly swapped strange experiences. Michael waited and eventually everyone went quiet again.

"Some of you even decided you must be in the wrong business," he went on. "After all, real angels never 'lose it.' Real angels are unfailingly beautiful, calm, and serene and know all the answers. Isn't that right?"

"Well, yeah," said someone.

"Rubbish," said Michael cheerfully. "An angel who has never experienced a second's doubt, an angel who never made a mistake, or was never tempted to tell a lie, would not be suitable for guardian angel training."

I sat up. Wow, I thought, I am *so* suitable!

"Your experiences were actually proof that you are ready to watch over a human being. With appropriate supervision, of course," he added, smiling.

My hands went clammy. "But this isn't like, our own personal human? I mean, we still have to work in teams, right?" I asked him.

Michael shook his head. "Guardian angels work strictly one-to-one."

"But you're always going on about teamwork," I blustered. "'No stars or heroes.' Isn't that what you're always saying?"

"That's exactly what I'm always saying," he agreed calmly. "I'm delighted it's finally sinking in."

I was not in the mood to be teased. "So—so how come you changed the rules?" I stuttered. "How come now it's about going to Earth all on your own, and baby-sitting some human stranger single-handed? Not to mention, ooh, protecting them from the Powers of Darkness! Frankly I don't think anyone in this hall is ready for that much responsibility." My voice was squeaky with fear.

Michael ignored my drama-queen tactics. "No one ever feels ready," he said firmly. "Angels become ready, by taking risks, by trusting that we will receive the help we need, exactly when we need it."

I rolled my eyes. "Oh yeah, the Angel Link, how could I forget. Have you actually tried to access the Link on Earth with the PODS, erm, I mean, the Opposition, breathing down your neck?"

"Many times," he said quietly. "Which is why we're issuing you all with these."

A junior agent stepped forward. Without a hint of a smile he held up a dinky little mobile phone. In a bored voice, he began to demonstrate its various functions, which I have to admit were quite impressive. Actually having something technical to concentrate on really helped calm me down. I didn't exactly stop being scared, but my panic definitely subsided into the background.

It was early evening by the time we left the Agency Tower. We were being sent off on our separate missions early next day. None of us felt like going back to school, so we stopped off at

Guru. Lola and I were too nervous to eat an actual meal, so we just ordered smoothies. But when our order came, Mo unloaded heaps of goodies from his tray.

"You'll need more than smoothies where you're going," he said firmly.

All the other customers were smiling at us and I went totally hot all over. That's the one thing about Heaven I can't get used to. Everyone knows your private business!

It didn't help that Orlando was sitting at the next table. Orlando literally looks like an angel, the dark-eyed kind you see in Italian paintings. He's also the school genius. Unfortunately I only tend to run into him when I'm breaking some major cosmic law, which doesn't exactly give a good impression.

With a little help from the boys, Lola and I managed to demolish most of Mo's tasty tidbits. I was going to ask her if she fancied sharing some of Guru's special passion-fruit pudding, when my surroundings flickered out of focus. I blinked but it got worse. I thought I might be getting some kind of weird angel migraine so I decided to call it a night.

"Have fun tomorrow, you guys!" I told my

mates. "Miss you already," I whispered to Lola. I meant it. I felt as if part of me was drifting away from her, like a kite with a broken string.

I closed the café door and the voices and laughter faded behind me. From now on, it's just you and the cosmos, Mel, I told myself.

I heard the door open again. Someone came out and I went tingly all over. "Mind if I walk back with you?" Orlando asked.

I gave him my coolest shrug. "I don't mind."

He peered up at the sky where the sunset had left streaks of tawny gold. "Feels like trying to watch two movies at once, doesn't it?" he commented sympathetically.

I was stunned. "How did you know?"

"It's a side-effect of GA work. You've become tuned to your human's wavelength. That's how you heard the Call. Now the vibes of his or her time and place are all mixed up with your reality."

"No wonder I feel so spaced," I breathed.

With humungous concentration, I managed to ignore my flickery visual disturbances and walk in a more or less straight line.

"So, have you done much erm, GA work?" I said, as if I habitually talked in initials.

"About four modules now."

I flashed him a cautious smile. "So if I pass this module, you know, without breaking any cosmic laws . . ."

"Like whacking a world-famous playwright." He grinned.

"Hey," I said. "How was I to know it was William Shakespeare? Like I was saying, if I get through the first module without a major screw-up, they'll give me tougher GA assignments, right? Is that it?"

"Why, do you think you'll like GA work?" Orlando seemed genuinely interested.

I tried to sound nonchalant. "Maybe. Ask me again when I get back."

We were walking past the Sanctuary. I glimpsed shining beings moving to and fro between the pillars. The Sanctuary angels devote their entire existence to healing. I could feel their tender vibes streaming through the twilight. It was so lovely I could have cried.

"Remember the first time you saw injured agents coming back from Earth?" Orlando said softly. "You asked me what kind of human would hurt an angel."

I'd been shocked to the core when Orlando

told me about the evil forces which deliberately try to sabotage our work on Earth. The Agency refers to them as the Opposition. My mates and I just call them the PODS, short for Powers of Darkness.

"I guess I'm the type who has to learn the hard way," I said ruefully.

Orlando's eyes were gentle. "You were just innocent."

I felt a little ache of loss. "You're right. I was. Until I met Brice."

The truth is, Brice and innocence don't exactly mix. It's like, even before we met, we had this embarrassing history. He worked for the PODS, at least he used to. To complicate things, he looked exactly like this boy I used to fancy at my old school. Until you saw his eyes, which were totally empty.

I ran into him on my first ever field trip to Earth, and by complete beginner's luck, got the better of him. Unfortunately bad-boy Brice wasn't your forgive-and-forget type. Like the Demon King in a tacky pantomime, he popped up during our mission to Tudor times and gave our buddy Reuben a horrifying beating. Lola and I only just got to Reubs in time. Thanks to the

Sanctuary angels, Reuben recovered from his injuries, but the memory still upset me.

"The guy's a total outlaw," I told Orlando angrily. "He isn't even a real PODS. He's an angel who changed sides. Can you believe that?"

His expression was annoyingly serene. "I heard he had his reasons."

I snorted. "Oh, please. We ran into him in the future, remember? He told us this big sob story and I wish he hadn't."

Orlando looked genuinely bewildered. "Why?"

"It's too confusing. I mean, is Brice a good guy who temporarily went bad, an evil joker pretending to be good, or just a lost little puppy who needs a home?" I tugged at my hair. "Aargh! I just want to forget about him."

Orlando has this unnerving ability to read my mind. "But you feel responsible for him at the same time," he suggested.

"I suppose," I admitted. "I mean, he sold his soul to the PODS purely to save his little brother from their evil Mafia-type family."

He succeeded too, with a bit of angelic cooperation. It's a long story, believe me. But just as Michael and everyone arrived to tie up any loose ends, Brice totally vanished. It's like he was ashamed to show his face. Obviously I hated the jerk as much as ever, but I couldn't help worrying about what would happen to him. When I tried asking Michael he just went into Yoda mode, something about taking the long-term view and trees eventually turning into diamonds.

I sighed. "Brice blew it with our Agency. He's blown it with the PODS. Where else is there?"

Orlando didn't answer and I realized we'd arrived back at my dorm.

"So, erm, where are you off to now?" I said awkwardly.

Orlando looked down at his trainers and I sneaked the opportunity to admire his beautiful eyelids. "I'm due down at the Angel Watch center."

"But that's in the complete opposite direction!"

"I know." Giving me one of his sweet enigmatic smiles, Orlando strolled off into the dark.

I stared after him wonderingly. Was it possible, after all our fights and misunderstandings, that this incredible boy actually *liked* me? A soppy smile spread over my face.

Then a chilling thought brought me back to

reality. In a few hours I was going on my first GA assignment and I had absolutely nothing to wear!

I hurtled up to my room and tried out every look you can think of: streetwise, funky, cute 'n' fluffy, until my bed was totally buried under clothes. Finally I plumped for my shocking pink Kung Fu Kitty T-shirt, teamed with bootleg jeans and suede sandals. I'd created the perfect look for today's guardian angel: stylish yet girly, caring yet seriously feisty.

I knew I wouldn't be able to sleep a wink, so I perched on the edge of my chair, clutching my flight bag and listening to my headphones. "You're not alone," I sang bravely. "You're not alone."

At last the Agency limo purred into the car park. I ran down, jumped into the front—and almost had a heart attack. Michael was in the driver's seat.

"Hi," he said calmly. "I thought we could talk on the way down."

I gulped. I could only think of one reason for Michael playing chauffeur. He was going to haul me over the coals for my outburst earlier that day. "If it's about my attitude," I quavered, "I'm really—"

He shook his head. "I wanted to talk about Brice."

Yeah, well I don't, okay?

"Oh, right," I said aloud.

Michael explained that he'd managed to track down my old enemy to his obscure cosmic hide-out. Since then they'd met up several times "on neutral ground," as Michael put it. I pictured the two of them sitting on some little rock out in space, the archangel and the boy with beautiful empty eyes, having some major discussion about good and evil.

To my surprise, I was okay with this. I was glad Michael was keeping an eye on Brice. That meant I totally needn't worry about him any-more.

"The dilemma is, what now?" He sighed. "We knew when we accepted him into the Academy that it wasn't going to be easy. But his soul scan was outstanding, so we decided to take the long-term view."

"Oh yeah, trees and diamonds," I remembered. "Too bad it didn't work out."

I love Michael to bits as you know, but I really wasn't in the mood to play cosmic agony aunt. In a few minutes I'd be alone on Earth, with just my wits and my mobile phone for protection, and the thought made me weak at the knees.

Michael suddenly looked apologetic. "Sorry, Melanie, you'll be wanting to know where you're going."

"Well . . ." I began doubtfully.

Then he told me and I screamed my head off!

"Omigosh, omigosh!" I burbled. "That is so cool!"

He smiled. "It is a fascinating period. An era of massive change and contradictions. You could say it's when modern times properly began."

I was trying to take it in. I couldn't believe it. I was going to what has to be the most exciting country in the world, during its most stylish era ever—1920s USA!

Chapter Three

IT WAS THREE O'CLOCK in the morning and I'd expected Departures to be deserted. But to my surprise hundreds of trainee GAs were milling around with their luggage.

I felt a rush of pride. We were all in this together. We had all been summoned by the same awesome cosmic force, and I felt so honored that I kept smiling at complete strangers!

Can you believe I had to join four separate queues to pick up all my Agency stuff? My 1920s info pack, my special Agency watch, my mobile, and finally my angel tags, the platinum discs we wear when we're on official Agency business.

Lola and I usually help each other fasten them, but this time I had to manage on my own. I was so nervous that I was still struggling with the clasp when the door of my portal slid shut. Al, my favorite maintenance guy, rapped on the glass and made me jump. "Ready?" he mouthed.

I gave Al and Michael a shaky thumbs-up. Next minute the portal lit up like the Fourth of July and I was catapulted out of Heaven.

I've done heaps of time-traveling since I've been at the Academy, but it's always a total miracle to witness Earth's entire history stream past in a matter of moments.

While I waited to land, I had a squint at my information pack, and discovered I was heading for the city of Philadelphia to watch over a girl called Honesty Bloomfield. I felt a happy little zing inside my heart. I just *knew* that Honesty was going to be really special. I sort of suspected she might be some kind of celebrity, like a child movie star or whatever.

Hang about, I thought, have they invented movies yet?

I riffled through my notes and was thrilled to find out that movie-making really took off in the Twenties. That's it! I thought excitedly. Honesty's this feisty girl who has dreams of being a big star, but she's from totally the wrong side of the tracks, so she needs my help to overcome her many obstacles and make her dream come true.

The colors outside the portal grew intensely

clear and bright. Any minute now, I'd be touching down. I counted under my breath. Four, three, two, *one*!

With a final burst of light, the portal vanished and I found myself all alone on planet Earth.

I gazed around at the sunny silent street with its flowering cherry trees and manicured gardens and my heart sank into my suede sandals. How could they *do* this to me? Everyone knows I'm a city girl. Suburbs, especially posh suburbs, are just not my style.

I squashed my negative thoughts. So what if it's the right side of the tracks, I scolded myself. Probably Honesty hates it too. Probably she's this major square peg, and you're here to help her find the courage to defy her uptight family and become an all-singing, all-dancing star of the silver screen.

This was such a cool scenario that I instantly cheered up.

My Agency watch beeped and I started to run through my landing procedure. I was just checking the prevailing thought levels, when I heard someone singing. I felt a tingle of angel electricity as I recognized the nickelodeon tune.

Two girls were coming down the street. The

younger girl was lolloping along like a playful puppy, really belting out the song, hideously off-key. Her sister was peering at a book through a pair of owlish spectacles, reading as she walked. They both wore dowdy school uniforms with hems trailing around their ankles and round felt hats like pork pies.

For the first time I got a good look at the first girl and felt the strangest chime inside my heart, as if two pieces of a puzzle had finally come together. At least, that's how the angel me was feeling. My inner bimbo was like, yippee! It's my future film star!

Honesty unfastened some white gates and gave her sister a nudge. "Rose," she prompted. "We're back."

"Uh-huh," mumbled Rose. She trudged up the drive, still reading, and Honesty lolloped happily after her.

They were heading for the grandest house in the street. It was one of those painted clapboard houses with a front porch, and it had a huge garden. I'm talking swimming pool and tennis courts, that kind of huge. Piano music was pouring from a downstairs window.

At this point, my angel self was going, it's

not Honesty's fault she was born into a humungously rich family, she could still be a really worthwhile person! But a doubting voice said—if she's got so much going for her, why would she need me?

Honesty opened the front door and Rose headed upstairs still reading, apparently finding her way by some kind of personal radar.

Honesty dumped her school bag down in the hall. She went bounding into a front parlor where a woman was playing the piano with a faraway expression. Honesty called to her over the torrent of sound. "Hi, Mama. I'm home."

The music stopped. "Well, hi, sweetheart!"

Honesty's mum was exceptionally pretty, with her fair hair swept up in smooth coils. She held out her arms and Honesty walked into them.

"How was your day, sugar?" Her mum's voice had a smoky southern lilt, like Scarlett in that old film *Gone with the Wind*.

"Okay, I guess. Only got a B+ in my math test though."

I stared at her. Only got a B+! I personally am ecstatic if I get a C!

"Nevermind, sugar," said her mum. "Everyone has off days." Her fingers strayed toward the piano keys, and I could tell she was dying to continue playing. "Why don't you run and ask Cissie to get you some milk and cookies?" she suggested.

Oh, whaaat! I thought. These people have servants!

Honesty hovered as if she had something on her mind. "Mama, did Papa say any more about buying a car? Every time I ask him, he says he's thinking about it. I don't understand what there is to think about. It's not like we don't have the money!"

Her mother gave a husky laugh. "Sweetheart, men are like mules. They won't budge unless they think it's all their own idea. Give him a few more weeks and he'll come round, I swear."

"It's not fair," Honesty complained. "We're the only kids in Philadelphia whose father is still stuck in the nineteenth century."

"Honesty, that's enough," said her mother firmly. "Your father is the hardest-working, biggest-hearted man I know and I will not allow you to criticize him this way."

Honesty turned bright red. "Sorry, Mama."

"You run and get those cookies," said her mum with a smile. "Dinner might be late tonight."

Honesty clomped off down the corridor, clearly

annoyed at not getting her own way. I followed, sniffing the air. Mmnn, vanilla and cinnamon, my all-time favorite aromas!

In the kitchen, trays of newly baked cookies were cooling by an open window. A tall black woman was helping a curly-haired little boy cut circles from leftover dough. There was a flour smudge on his nose and the tip of his tongue stuck out while he worked. I grinned. He looked just like my little sister does when she's concentrating.

The kitchen was pretty and homey in a retro kind of way, with its gleaming pots and pans, an old-fashioned range, and a low sink with a scrubbed wooden draining board. A corner of the kitchen was occupied by a monster refrigerator. I had the feeling fridges were, like, the latest hi-tech invention.

The little boy suddenly caught sight of Honesty. His face lit up. "You're home! I baked cookies for you, look!" He peered anxiously at the lumpy gray shapes on his baking tray. "Cissie says they'll look better when they're cooked, didn't you, Cissie?"

She grinned. "They're fine, Clem honey. You

want me to finish these off for you?"

"Okay," Clem said promptly. He slipped off his chair and ran to bury his face in his sister's stomach. "I missed you, sis," he said happily.

"Quit it, Clem," Honesty complained. "You're getting flour over me. Anyway, little boys don't do baking. That's for little girls."

I understood exactly why Honesty was being so mean. She hadn't got her own way about the car, so now she was taking it out on Clem. And I know it's not very angelic, but when I saw her brother's hurt little face, I wanted to smack her one. Doesn't this girl know how lucky she is? I fumed. Doesn't she realize some kids would kill to be in her position?

I'm not saying I wanted to actually, like, *be* Honesty, being welcomed home by a piano-playing mother, a cookie-baking maid, and a cute little brother. It was *my* family I wanted. My mum and my funny little sister, Jade, and my lovely stepdad, Des. What I missed was being human and alive.

But I couldn't exactly criticize Honesty, because when I lived on Earth I was just the same. There was always that mysterious missing "something" that stopped my life from being perfect. That gorgeous little skirt from Top Shop, or a must-have CD.

It's agony seeing someone make the same mistakes you made, so I took myself off to explore the rest of the house.

The minute I was alone again, it struck me that Honesty's house had a really unusual atmosphere, intensely sweet and peaceful. It might sound stupid, but I felt as if the house was *waiting* for something. The feeling was disturbingly familiar, but though I racked my brains, I couldn't seem to remember why.

I passed through the parlor where Honesty's mum was still playing her Beethoven or whatever. There was a vase of lilacs on the piano. I stopped to breathe in their gorgeous scent and noticed a photograph of Honesty's parents' wedding day. *Aah,* I thought. They both looked desperately young and nervous and totally head over heels in love.

There was a fancy studio portrait of an older boy I guessed to be Honesty's big brother. Mmm! I thought approvingly. Definitely inherited his daddy's looks.

I flitted invisibly up the huge staircase and

went into the girls' bedroom, where Rose sat on her bed, glued to her book.

I peeped over her shoulder. What's got her so gripped? I thought. A fruity love story? A juicy diary? But Rose's reading material totally took me by surprise. It was all about ancient Egypt: old tombs and mummies' curses, pure Indiana Jones! I was so impressed!

I roamed around the girls' bedroom, nosing into cupboards and peering at shelves. I told myself that I was not snooping, but simply gathering information. Somewhere in this room was the evidence that revealed Honesty's secret intention of breaking out of the 'burbs and into international filmstardom.

Except that it wasn't. My search revealed precisely *nada*. No tap shoes, sheet music, or inspiring movie posters. And the dreary garments in Honesty's wardrobe betrayed no hint of a creative spirit trying to break free.

You'd think she'd have *one* little drop-waisted Charleston dress, I thought crossly.

I heard a metallic jangle somewhere in the house, and Honesty's mum started talking to someone. I got the feeling she was incredibly excited about something, because her intonation became heaps more southern.

I sighed. I had now inspected all of Honesty's worldly possessions, except for a stash of notebooks at the back of a drawer. To judge from the threats on the covers (KEEP YOUR NOSE OUT OF MY STUFF OR YOU'LL DIE IN AGONY. YES, ROSE BLOOMFIELD, THAT MEANS YOU!), they were Honesty's journals and there was no way I was stooping to read someone's secret diaries, thank you very much.

I was now officially flummoxed. I had no idea what a real guardian angel would do next. I thought of calling the GA helpline and asking for tips, but I'd only just got here. So I settled down at a little old-fashioned bureau, dug out my fact pack and did some research.

I found out that only a few years ago the First World War was blasting the old world to smithereens. The western world had witnessed too much horror and people couldn't handle it. You can't exactly blame them. They didn't want to feel guilty for surviving when so many millions had died. They didn't want to know how terrible humans could be to each other. They wanted to forget all that. They wanted to have fun. So when the Twenties arrived, everyone went crazy. Good girls hacked off their hems, painted their faces, and turned into bad but gorgeous flappers. People danced for days without sleeping, and held mad competitions like who could shove the most sticks of gum in their mouths, or swallow the most live goldfish. In America this urgent need to party was complicated by something called the Prohibition law. In other words, alcohol was basically banned. Of course, this only made people more desperate to get hold of it.

If I shut my eyes, I could actually feel that frantic glittery Twenties spirit, surfing on a sea of darkness and chaos. I'd always imagined the Twenties to be like one long frothy bubble bath. I'd never thought about the deadly PODS vibes under the froth. Omigosh, the poor things, I thought. They're all living for the moment like beautiful butterflies.

And then I thought, yeah, right, butterflies! In Hollywood maybe. But I was stuck in some stodgy Philadelphia suburb with a little diary-keeping rich girl who, let's face it, was not ideal butterfly material.

I heard footsteps pounding upstairs. Honesty burst in, her face blazing with excitement. "Rose!

You'll never guess what happened. Papa just called Mama on the telephone, and—"

"And obviously you eavesdropped," said Rose drily.

"Rose! I'm telling you the most thrilling news since the invention of moving pictures! He's actually gone and bought—"

Rose jumped up so fast, her little spectacles actually fell off her nose. "I don't believe it!" she shrieked. "Papa's bought a car!"

"He's on his way to pick it up. He's driving it home!"

The girls threw their arms around each other, squealing happily.

I wanted to be thrilled for them, but the strange sweet vibe was growing steadily more intense and I was having my two-movies-at-once sensation again. Something was happening to someone in this family. I could feel it with every one of my angel senses.

"You have to pretend to be surprised," Honesty was saying. "Daddy will be so disappointed if we don't act surprised."

"Act! I won't have to act!" Rose laughed. "I'm ecstatic."

Honesty flew over to an old-fashioned gramophone with a shiny brass horn and cranked a handle. A scratchy voice floated out of the horn. "Put another nickel in, in the nickelodeon." This was obviously their fave tune of the moment.

The girls started dancing the Charleston, flouncing their skirts and showing their big white knickers. Clem and Cissie rushed in to see what on earth was going on. Honesty grabbed her brother and whirled him around the room. Rose grabbed Cissie, and instead of being annoyed, Cissie kicked up her heels and did this wicked little dance step.

When movie characters get overexcited like this, something terrible always happens. But I tried to tell myself that this was real life, not Hollywood. There was no reason the Bloomfields couldn't live happily ever after. But by this time, I think I'd sussed that "happy ever after" was not an option.

As the tragedy inched closer, I felt an invisible cosmic gateway opening. The sweetness grew unbearably beautiful and I suddenly knew when I'd felt it before. It was during my last day on Earth, as angels gathered like invisible birds to guide me back to Heaven.

I knew then that someone was going to die. I'd got here just in time to see Honesty's old world blown to smithereens. And there was nothing I could do about it.

Chapter Four

THE GIRLS CRACKED car jokes right up to dinnertime. How Mr. Bloomfield was so old-fashioned he was probably still figuring out how to hitch the new Model A Ford to the horse, or how he was so thrilled with his new toy, he'd gone for a spin via the Rockies on his way home.

But when eight o'clock came and went and he still failed to appear, the atmosphere started getting strained.

"You'd better dish up, Cissie," said Honesty's mum.

But no one could manage to eat Cissie's good roast chicken and mashed potatoes, and in the end she took the food away, shaking her head.

I found their reactions slightly surprising. My stepdad could have been, like, five hours late and no one would have raised an eyebrow. Des is the world's worst timekeeper. Mum used to say he operated on 'Desmond time.' But I got the feeling that if Mr. Bloomfield said he'd be back by eight, then he was back.

It was dark when the police car drove up. Two grim-faced cops came to the door and Cissie showed them into the parlor. The children clustered around their mother. Clem was shivering like a puppy. He knew something terrible had happened.

They'd sent a young cop and an old cop, just like in the movies. The young guy was looking everywhere but at the Bloomfields. The old cop cleared his throat. "Mrs. Grace Bloomfield, I'm sorry to have to—"

Rose burst into tears. Honesty went white and ran out of the room.

In those days, they didn't make you take a test before they let you loose on the road. Drivers just picked up the necessary know-how as they tootled along in the traffic. Sadly, Honesty's father never got the chance. He hit a truck ten minutes after he left the Ford garage. The cops said he died instantly.

Honesty's mother roamed around the house all that night, sick with grief. Once she came into the girls' room in her nightdress and watched them as they lay sleeping. But that was the one and only time I saw Grace Bloomfield lose control. When she came down to breakfast next morning, she was deathly pale but totally composed. "I can get through this so long as I don't let myself think," I heard her tell Cissie.

"That's right, Mizz Grace," agreed Cissie. "You got your whole life for thinking. Right now, you got to survive."

I'd spent the night radiating angelic vibes to everyone in the household. In my opinion the entire family needed heavenly support.

Later I wondered if I'd got it wrong. If I'd concentrated on Honesty like I was supposed to, I might have been quicker to spot the signs. That first day when she came down to breakfast and said in a toneless voice, "Oh, great, waffles!"—that wasn't normal, but I refused to see it.

Rose had been crying so hard, her face looked as if it had been stung by swarms of bees. And Clem clung to his mama's skirts as if he was terrified she'd be next to disappear. But Honesty heaped her plate with ham, eggs, and hash browns, drenched her waffles with maple syrup, shoveled it all down like a zombie, and said, "See you later," and pushed back her chair.

Rose peered out between her swollen eyelids. "What are you doing?"

"Going to school," said Honesty in her new zombie voice. "Same as usual."

Her mother put her arms around her. "That's very brave, sugar, but you don't have to go to school today. . . ."

Honesty wriggled free. "I do. I've got a test in geography."

Grace stood firm. But by the end of the day, I bet she wished she'd let Honesty take her stupid test after all, because she was a complete nightmare.

When Honesty heard that her brother Lenny was coming back from medical school for the funeral, she just said, "Great. We've got to share the house with Lenny's stinky socks." Rose said they'd have to go into town to buy clothes for the funeral and Honesty snapped, "You can dress like a Sicilian widow if you want to. It's not like Papa's going to care. When you're dead, you're dead."

Honesty had had a total personality change. She was hardly recognizable as the sweet goofy girl who hugged her mum, yelled at her baby brother, and flaunted her big knickers dancing the Charleston.

And there was another thing. When I first met Honesty, her thoughts were so easy to read, she might as well as have yelled them through a megaphone. But now she was putting out no thoughtwaves whatsoever.

Lenny came home for the funeral and everyone else rushed to the door to meet him. They cried and hugged each other and generally behaved like human beings. But Honesty didn't even bother to come downstairs.

When the family met up for the evening meal, Lenny tried to put his arms around her, but she pulled away. "People die every day, you know," she said coldly. "You don't have to make a big production out of it."

That night I took my mobile out of my flight bag. I got as far as punching in the GA code. Then I thought, I'll give it until after the funeral. Then she'll start to grieve properly and she'll be really sad but basically okay.

Honesty's dad must have been well respected in Philadelphia, because absolutely loads of people came to the funeral. Though I didn't see any members of their families as such, like cousins or grandparents. It was more business associates with their wives.

Grace kept glancing nervously around the church as if someone important was missing.

I heard Lenny whisper, "Probably he's sick."

"Then why didn't he call?" Grace whispered back. "He didn't even send flowers. He's supposed to be his best friend for heaven's sake."

Honesty had this annoying nervous smirk on her face.

Finally Rose couldn't stand it. "What's so funny?" she asked.

Honesty shrugged. "I was wondering what Papa would make of being buried in a church."

Rose hissed, "You know Papa didn't care about all that stuff."

Honesty gave her a poisonous look. "We don't know any such thing *actually*, Rose Bloomfield. Papa's ancestors must be turning in their graves."

She made it sound as if her father was a vampire or something. Funeral or no funeral, this girl is getting too weird, I thought uneasily.

After the funeral, Grace invited all the mourners back to the house. Everyone stood around the front parlor, making agonizing small talk.

I noticed Grace was still watching the door. I heard her ask Lenny, "Did you try Jack Coltraine's number again?"

He nodded. "Still no reply."

This news seemed to worry Grace. "I'd appreciate it if you could just keep trying, will you?"

"Of course, Mama," he said.

Jack Coltraine never did pick up the phone. That's because he had taken off for Havana with all of Honesty's father's money. Next day, the family lawyer confirmed Grace's worst suspicions. Jack had been creaming off the business profits, stashing them in safety deposit boxes in his wife's name. In a matter of days, the Bloomfields' lives had totally turned upside down. They'd lost everything, including their home. All Grace stood to inherit now were her husband's debts.

That night Lenny came into the girls' room and I heard him and Rose talking. Honesty stayed huddled silently under her covers, giving off such minimal vibes, I don't think they even remembered she was there.

I was shocked to hear Lenny say, "I'll really miss Papa, but in a weird way it's set me free. Being a doctor was his dream, not mine."

"So what's yours, Len?" Rose's voice was still snuffly from crying.

"Don't laugh," he said awkwardly. "I want to be a stuntman. I met this actor on the train. He said there are great opportunities in the film industry for young guys like me, who aren't afraid to take risks."

Rose was disgusted. "You've had this expensive education and you want to throw it all away just so you can fall off horses and get brain damage! Have you any idea how lucky you are to be a boy? I'd do anything to go to college. But I'm a girl, so everyone assumes I'll just marry a nice doctor. Aargh!"

"You won't have to get married for years yet. I'm sure Papa would want you girls to finish your education."

Rose gave him a bleak smile. "Nice theory, Len. Where's the money coming from?"

"I think Mama should ask her family for help. They own some big plantation in the south, don't they? They must have loads of dough."

Rose shook her head. "Mama's family is a taboo subject. Remember how she used to clam up when we asked about them?"

"I know, but it's the best I can think of," Lenny said miserably.

But the next day, to their astonishment, Grace brought the subject up herself.

"I have reached a very difficult decision. I

have been lying awake, racking my brains, and I cannot see an alternative. I have a little jewelry, enough to buy train tickets with some left over for emergencies."

"Mama," said Rose. "What are you talking about?"

Grace seemed to be talking to herself. "I was so young when I left home. People can change. Whatever happened, you're still his flesh and blood. I'm sure when your grandaddy actually sees you, he'll want to help. We'll pack a few necessities, and the lawyers can see to the rest."

I noticed Honesty slip out of the room while her mother was still talking. I hurried after her and found her in her bedroom removing her diaries from the drawer.

She tore the pages from the notebooks, stuffed them into the tiny fireplace and dropped a lighted match into the grate. When her diaries were reduced to a heap of curling black ash, Honesty lifted down a suitcase from the top of the wardrobe and started to pack.

She folded bloomers, chemises, blouses, and pinafores; put them into her case and carefully fastened both catches. Then she put on her horrible coat and hat, seated herself on a hard wooden chair and stayed there, staring into space, until the taxi came and the Bloomfields left their home forever.

I left with them, so I saw that Honesty didn't once look back. She just stared straight ahead, humming tunelessly. I knew then that this was going to be the toughest assignment of my angelic career.

Chapter Five

IN HONESTY'S DAY, a first-class train carriage looked exactly like your great granny's front parlor, right down to the tablecloth with fancy fringes. They look cute in movies, but in reality they ponged of dust and coal fumes and men's cigars, not to mention human sweat. People weren't too big on personal hygiene back then.

After he'd stashed everyone's luggage, Lenny went into the corridor. He pulled down the window and watched the Philadelphia skyline disappearing into the distance.

Grace had brought a pack of cards and started to build a house for Clem. Rose was curled up in a corner seat, reading as usual. Honesty stared at her fingernails, then muttered, "I'm going to get a soda."

I hurried after her along the swaying corridor. The soda was just an excuse, because Honesty walked right through the dining car and out the other side. These carriages were crowded with tired men and women sitting on hard benches instead of plushy upholstery, and there were ratty cardboard suitcases on the luggage racks instead of leather.

I was surprised to feel my skin prickling like crazy. This usually means there are other angels in the vicinity. Sure enough, two carriages down, I spotted that giveaway cosmic glow. An earth angel was sitting calmly among the paying passengers. She wore a shabby Twenties coat and a cute little cloche hat trimmed with a faded silk rose. I felt so proud of my profession, I can't tell you. The humans had no idea they were sharing their railway carriage with an invisible celestial agent, but from their peaceful expressions I knew they were responding to her angelic vibes.

The angel and I gave each other a brief wave, one agent to another. Then I hurtled breathlessly after Honesty.

Our train shook and shuddered as another train roared past. There was a flash of fire, and I glimpsed the driver furiously stoking the boiler. Steam billowed past the windows, like special effects on pop videos.

I heard snatches of talk from the passengers. An old man was complaining, "You know the thing about America? Everyone is always rushing someplace else." And I heard a salesman boasting, "Nowadays it's not enough to sell sausages. You got to sell the *sizzle* too!"

In the last carriage, tough-looking hoodlums in slouch hats were playing cards. Honesty stood watching until one of them noticed her and said humorously, "Beat it, kid. Didn't your mama tell you gambling was wrong?"

Honesty rolled her eyes. "I'm just watching. Anyway, what my mama doesn't know won't hurt her."

He made her a mocking bow. "Step inside, sister."

The old Honesty wouldn't dream of behaving like this, but the new Honesty seemed determined to walk on the wild side. Occasionally, the guys passed around a brown paper bag, and took swigs from a bottle concealed inside. They jokingly offered it to Honesty, but she said coldly, "Haven't you heard? That stuff is illegal."

"I was just going to send Lenny to look for you. What took you so long?" Grace asked her when we returned.

"I was talking to some interesting people for a change," Honesty said rudely. "You don't think I'm going to stay cooped up in here all the way to Georgia, do you?"

After lunch, Honesty went to sleep and I watched the vast landscape flow past. Occasionally a shabby little railroad town flew by. Ragged kids waved from the fields. Clearly our train was the big event of their day.

For no apparent reason the train began to slow down and eventually came to a standstill. At first, I thought we'd stopped beside some kind of massive garbage dump. Then I saw it was a little hobo town, a settlement of tumbledown shacks and improvised tents that had grown up beside the tracks. A couple of guys were having an argument. An older guy was slumped by a campfire with his head in his hands. I could see his toes sticking through the broken ends of his boots. Dirty little kids ran around half naked, despite the cold. One of them was still just a baby. A woman was stirring a pot over the fire. She was so thin her clothes hung off her shoulders like a sack. Desperate feelings welled up inside me. The kind that make you go, "Why bother? This life is just too hard."

Fortunately, I'm an angel, so I soon sussed that these weren't my personal feelings. They weren't anyone's personal feelings, in fact. Originally they were probably an evil freebie from the PODS. Now deadly PODS vibes hung over the makeshift settlement like fog, and the wretched inhabitants had no choice but to inhale and exhale them with every breath. The PODS really have some sick strategies for making humans do their work for them.

The baby toddled up to the woman and pulled at her skirts. The train gave its mournful wail and she picked up the baby and turned to gaze at us as we moved off, as if all her hopes and dreams were leaving on our train.

As the train gathered speed, I did something I should have done days ago. I got out my Agency mobile and called up the GA helpline.

I couldn't help smiling as I waited for someone to pick up. It would be so cool to say, "Hi, it's me, I'm on a train!" Then I heard the helpline worker's voice and went hot to the roots of my hair.

"Finally!" said Orlando. "We've been expecting you to call for days."

Did it have to be him? I thought. Couldn't I

just once talk to Orlando when everything is going well?

I reminded myself that I was a bona fide celestial trouble-shooter, and calmly updated Orlando on everything that had happened.

"I sit up all night, beaming her vibes," I finished up. "But nothing seems to get through. She's totally locked inside herself and I'm scared she's going to do something stupid."

"You think she's a suicide risk?" he asked.

I felt a stab of worry. "I don't think she'd deliberately—"

Rose dropped her book with a crash. I saw that people were running out into the corridor. I looked to see what had got everyone so excited and gave an unprofessional shriek. "Yikes! I've got to go!"

Thundering down a hillside toward us were hordes of Indian braves. As I reached the corridor, a mob of cowboys came galloping from behind the trees and they started having this major shoot-out. Horses reared and cowboys and Indians fell sprawling on the ground in horrifically gruesome positions.

This is terrible! I thought. People are killing each other, and I'm the only angel in the area.

I must do something!

Then an old truck came in sight with an old-fashioned movie camera on the top and I went limp with relief.

A tubby little man got out of the truck. He started bellowing through a megaphone and suddenly the whole scene rewound itself. All the dead horses, cowboys, and Indians miraculously came back to life and went scrambling back to their original positions, and the truck reversed madly out of the shot.

I felt like *such* a ditz. I could see now that the braves were nothing like real-life Native Americans, just white stuntmen in crude costumes and make-up.

The other passengers went back to their seats, but Lenny couldn't seem to move. He stayed glued to the train window until the actors were microscopic dots. Then he leaned his forehead on the dirty glass and closed his eyes, as if he was replaying the stuntmen's cheesy death throes in his mind.

The train tracks curved and divided and began to run along beside a river, a river that was totally unlike any I'd ever seen in England. It was vast, like the sea. Huge steamers chugged along like floating palaces, their paddles churning up the muddy river water. I've never seen anything so romantic as those riverboats. Their glitzy big-hearted names sounded like song lyrics to me: *Delta Queen, Heart of Georgia, Memphis Belle . . .*

The sun had started to set, and a path of gold and crimson rippled across the surface of the water. Honesty's mother pulled down the window, letting in the hot, damp, sweet-smelling air. From the expression on her face, I knew we had reached the south. Grace seemed delighted to be back in her home state—but I could sense the tension underneath, as if she secretly dreaded meeting her parents again after so many years.

My mobile went off in my bag. It was Orlando checking if everything was okay. I explained sheepishly about the shoot-out being a movie stunt, and he said, "What's that in the background?"

The train had just let out one of its plaintive wails, so I said, "You mean the train?"

"No, the music."

"Oh, it's some guys on a riverboat playing jazz." I held the phone up to the window so he could hear.

"Wish I was there," he said. "It sounds amazing."

I gazed out at the boat chugging past in the southern dusk. Suddenly its decks lit up with hundreds of tiny fairy lights. And I said softly, "It is so sublime you would not believe . . ."

Next morning the sun rose over cotton fields. It was barely dawn, and already sweating black men and women were working among the rows of fluffy cotton plants. A look of strain came over Grace's face.

Lenny and Rose were in the corridor talking in low voices. Rose looked upset so I went out to see what was going on.

"I'll make sure you get there safely, then I'm going to find those filmmakers and make them give me a job. I'm going to get into the movie business, Rose." Lenny sounded desperate. "You see if I don't. I'm a man. It's time I made my way in the world."

She gave a bitter little laugh. "A big man, playing cowboys! Bang bang you're dead! Oh, a really big man!"

I could see she was trying not to cry. Lenny said earnestly, "Rosie, we're not so different.

You're crazy about the past. Well, I'm just as crazy about modern times. Movies are where it's all happening. I've got to do it, sis!"

And Rose sniffed bravely and patted his back and said, "It's okay, Len. It's okay. We'll be okay."

Lenny kept his word. He came with them to the gates of the fine old plantation house where Honesty's mother had been born and brought up, then he hugged them all.

Everyone else watched forlornly as Lenny trudged back down the road in the shimmering noonday heat. But Honesty kept her head down, kicking sullenly at the dirt.

Grace took a deep breath. "Let's go meet your granddaddy," she said to Clem. "See if time has improved the old buzzard any."

And then she gasped. "Oh, my stars, it's Isaac!"

A barefoot black man with tufts of silver in his hair was coming down the porch steps. He looked as if he couldn't believe his eyes. "Mizz Grace?"

Grace ran and threw her arms around him. "Isaac, I have missed you *so* much!" Both of them had tears on their faces. "So how's Celestine?" she said eagerly.

Isaac's voice was so sorrowful, he almost seemed to be singing. "She passed, Mizz Grace. She passed. It's just me and the children now." He tried to smile. "Got me eight little grandbabies, can you believe that? Two of the girls work for your mama and daddy." He yelled into the house. "Dorcas, come out here." And Isaac's granddaughter came running out.

In my opinion, she was way too young to be working as anyone's maid, but apparently they did things differently down here. Dorcas was wearing a prim white cap and apron, but like Isaac she didn't seem to have any shoes.

"Mizz Grace is back," Isaac told her. His granddaughter gasped and a look passed between them. I thought, uh-oh.

Dorcas showed Grace and her children to a sunny terrace where Grace's parents were having breakfast.

Grace said nervously, "Hello Mama, Daddy."

There was a moment when any normal parent would have jumped up and hugged their long-lost child, but there was just this electric silence. Then her father dabbed his mouth with a napkin and said, "Why Grace, this is most unexpected. What brings you here?"

Honesty stepped forward. "If you must know, my papa got hit by a truck," she said in her zombie voice. "And his sleazeball partner vamoosed with all of Mama's money."

Rose looked appalled. "Honesty, for Heaven's sake."

"But that *is* why we're here," she said, all innocent. "You don't think we'd be sponging off our rich relations if we had a choice?"

Grace gave Honesty a look that would have reduced any normal child to a quivering jelly. "Please forgive my daughter," she said quietly. "This is not an easy time for us."

Her father ignored her and turned to Rose. Suddenly he was all folksy southern charm. "So what's your name, pumpkin?"

"She's Rose," piped Clem. "I'm Clem and this is Honesty."

"And honesty is obviously a quality dear to your sister's heart," said their grandfather, as if Honesty was invisible. "But when she grows a little wiser, I hope she will also learn the value of simple southern courtesy."

Grace's mother tinkled a bell and Dorcas ran in and bobbed a scared curtsey. Someone ought to tell these old relics that slavery's over, I thought angrily.

"Get my grandchildren's room ready," Grace's

mother drawled. "They can have Miss Grace's old room for now."

Rose looked puzzled. "But where will Mama sleep?"

"We'll talk about that later, dear." Their grandmother dingled the bell again and an even younger maid rushed in. "Take my grandchildren upstairs and run their baths," she said in that same languid tone. "They want to freshen up after their long journey."

The children reluctantly followed the maid into the house. Something felt distinctly off, so I thought I'd better stay with Grace and find out what was going on.

It's a good thing I did. As soon as Grace was alone with her parents, her father said coldly, "I'm sure you understand that it is quite impossible for you to stay here." He made it sound as if this was a reasonable thing to say to your own daughter.

Grace looked as if he'd struck her. "You're sending us away?"

"Just you, Grace," he said in the same cold reasonable voice. "The children can stay."

Grace opened her mouth but couldn't seem to find her voice.

"It's not as if they look Jewish," Grace's mother said brightly. "No one need ever know."

Oh, no *way*, I thought incredulously. No wonder she never came back home. These old monsters disapproved of Grace for marrying a Jew!

"I suggest you leave tonight, after the children are in bed," her father went on. "That way you'll avoid distressing them with overly emotional farewells."

Grace was breathing fast. "*Avoid* distressing them? My children have already lost their father, you can't possibly—"

Her father talked over her. "We'll simply tell everyone that you and the unfortunate Mr. Bloomfield died in the same tragic car wreck." He opened a drawer and pulled out a checkbook. "Don't worry, I'm not sending you away penniless."

"We can give them so many advantages, you see," wittered her mother. "Education, money, breeding."

"Yes, everything, Mama," Grace whispered.

"Yeah, right," I muttered angrily. "Everything but love."

Personally, I'd have just emptied the pitcher of orange juice over their heads, ice cubes and all.

Grace was normally a very strong-minded woman, but now she was back in her childhood home, all the fight had suddenly gone out of her. She'd lost faith in herself, and now she was starting to believe their poisonous lies.

That evening Grace came to kiss her children good night.

Honesty said pleadingly, "Mama, I don't like it here. Can we leave in the morning?"

She said it in her real voice, not the zombie one, but Grace didn't seem to hear. Actually Honesty's mother sounded like a sleepwalker herself. "It's bound to be strange at first, sugar, but you know your granddaddy can give you all a great deal."

"I've seen what he can give me, Mama," said Honesty, "and I would personally prefer to have rabies." And she pulled the covers over her head.

On an unconscious level, Grace's children totally sussed that their mother was planning to leave them. But they didn't know it for sure, so they couldn't beg her to stay. There was just all this silent agony going on. I beamed angel vibes at that family like crazy, but despite all my efforts, Grace Bloomfield crept out of the house about an hour later.

I know Clem felt her go because he immediately woke up and started to cry. Rose took him into bed with her. Without a word, Honesty climbed in beside him, and the three children huddled like orphans in Rose's king-sized bed. Eventually Clem went back to sleep still quivering with sobs. But both the sisters lay awake under the slowly rotating blades of the ceiling fan, completely unable to mention that their sole surviving parent had just left them forever.

I was desperately concerned for Honesty. If her father's death had turned her into a zombie, then losing her mum would probably tip Honesty right over the edge.

I groped in my flight bag, trying to find my mobile—and then I noticed some branches outside the window starting to shake. The window creaked open and someone climbed over the sill.

I heard a soft laugh. "I used to climb up and down that old magnolia all the time. Papa would lock me in and I'd be out of this window and cycling off to meet some boy, before he'd even reached the foot of our stairs."

Rose snapped on the light. "Mama? Have you gone crazy?" she said shakily. Clem sat up rubbing his eyes.

"No, sugar, I have just regained my sanity," said Grace. "I got as far as the crossroads, then I said to myself, 'Grace, those old dinosaurs have got you hopelessly confused, just like they always did. You know you can't live without those precious babies. Now go and get them out of there.'"

She gathered her children into her arms and Clem clung to her tearfully.

"Mama, how will we manage?" said Rose anxiously.

Grace seemed to have it all worked out. "Remember my cousin, Louella, in San Francisco?"

"The one who was mixed up in that big scandal!" Rose sounded shocked.

"I admit that Louella is a law unto herself," said Grace. "But she runs a successful dressmaking business and I'm sure she'll give me a job. Will you take your chance and come to California with me?" Her voice faltered. "Unless you'd rather—"

Rose flung her arms around her mother. "Of *course* we're coming with you, Mama!"

Clem's eyes went wide. "We're going to California—without Lenny?"

Grace gave him a hug. "Your brother's a smart

boy. He'll find us when he wants to."

The children scrambled into their clothes. Grace climbed out of the window first and they tossed down their bags to her. Clem slithered down the magnolia like a little monkey and Grace caught him at the bottom. Rose and Honesty went next, then me.

In the darkness the smell of magnolias was suddenly overpowering. The night was shrill with crickets, sounding exactly like tinny wind-up music boxes.

I saw Isaac watching from a shadowy veranda as Grace and her children crept around the side of the house. He didn't say anything but I sensed he'd known all along that his Miss Grace wouldn't abandon her babies. Actually I got the feeling Isaac knew too much about what went on in this family. So much he could hardly sleep at nights, just sat up in his creaky old rocker, looking at the stars and humming softly to himself.

Chapter Six

ON BAD DAYS WE WALKED. On good days we hitched a ride in the back of some farmer's truck or rickety horse-drawn wagon. Most days we did a bit of both. Just once, the Bloomfields accepted a lift in a shiny new Model A Ford. But after five minutes Grace had to ask the driver to stop. They barely got out in time before Honesty spewed her lunch everywhere. I wasn't totally surprised. She'd turned white as chalk the moment the driver pulled up. Being Honesty, she denied that her travel sickness was in any way connected with her father's accident, just as she denied that she screamed out in her sleep night after night. But I think Grace knew the real reason, because after that the family stuck purely to wagons and pickups.

But one sweltering afternoon, Clem was too tired to walk, and no one had the energy to carry him. So Grace and the children waited in the lengthening shadows of some lime trees, in the hope they'd get a lift to the next town. But no vehicles passed.

The first stars were coming out as a horse-drawn farm wagon pulled up. A young black guy looked down at them. He seemed oddly alarmed to see the family standing there in the dark. He glanced around. "I'm bettin' you ain't from around these parts," he said in a low voice. "Else you'd know it's dangerous to be out here after sundown."

I could feel pure physical fear pulsing off him. Omigosh, I thought. They must have some southern serial killer around here or something.

Then I got it. This man wasn't scared of some mad axe murderer. He was scared of Grace. He was terrified that someone would see him talking to a white lady and jump to the wrong conclusion. On the other hand, he felt totally unable to leave her and her kids stranded out in the sticks at the mercy of any passing local nutter.

"I'd better take you folks into Bournville. Better hide yourselves in the back though," he added in a humorous voice. "Won't do your reputation no good to be seen with a negro."

I saw him wonder if he'd gone too far. But Grace gave him one of her warm smiles. "I think our reputation can stand it," she told him. "But the back of the wagon will suit us just fine."

For over an hour we bumped over potholes in the dark, which gave me plenty of time to digest what had just happened. I don't mind telling you, I was finding racial attitudes in the American south of the Twenties deeply bewildering. I mean, slavery had been made illegal here, like, decades ago, yet this guy clearly expected nothing but trouble from mixing with whites.

The man stopped his horses on the edge of town. He came around to the back, holding up a storm lantern. "Where you folks headed?"

"California," said Clem, blinking in the sudden light.

"I meant where you stopping tonight?" he asked Grace.

"I have no idea!" She saw the man's concerned expression and laughed. "We'll be fine. We always are. Erm, thank you for the lift, Mr. . . . ?"

The guy looked startled. I could tell he wasn't used to white people calling him mister. "Glass," he said. "The name's Nathan Glass."

"Are we at California yet?" Clem whimpered.

Nathan sighed and I could see him wondering what he'd got himself into. "Guess I'd better take you to Peaches's place," he said reluctantly. "That's if you don't mind walking some?"

I could see Clem droop at the very thought. Nathan handed the lantern to Rose. "But you can ride, little man!" He swung Clem up onto his shoulders, laughing, then took back his lantern.

We followed him across a field and into the woods. If it hadn't been for Nathan's lantern it would have been pitch dark. We must have walked for half an hour, hurrying in and out of the trees. It was marshy in places and the local frogs kept up this monotonous backing track, interrupted by the occasional eerie cry of a night bird.

So far as I could tell there wasn't a house for miles. Don't tell me Peaches lives in a tree, I thought. Then I stopped in my tracks, frowning. I was in the middle of nowhere, but I was picking up an incredibly buzzy vibe, the kind you get when loads of people are grooving to the max.

Uh-oh, I thought. This is not a good time to start hallucinating, Melanie.

Nathan gave a throaty chuckle. "What can you hear?"

"Crickets?" said Rose in an exhausted voice.

"No, it's music!" said Clem, jigging about on Nathan's shoulders.

"The blues," Grace corrected him softly. "Someone's playing blues."

"Peaches runs a speakeasy out here," Nathan explained. "Just a shack and a few barrels of moonshine. But we reckon the music is as good as anything they get at the Cotton Club."

"Will there be any food?" asked Clem hopefully.

A few minutes later we emerged in a large clearing and I saw a rickety wooden shack. Hazy light leaked out from between the planks. I couldn't just hear the blues by this time—I could feel it, tingling up through the soles of my feet and into my belly. The shack was literally vibrating from the exuberant partying inside!

There was a break in the music and I heard a woman's teasing voice, then a roar of laughter. Nathan rapped on a little barred window. It slid open and an eye squinted out through a fog of cigarette smoke.

"Tell Peaches she's got company!" said Nathan.

The door opened and he bundled us inside.

There was a moment's astonished silence. Then someone said sarcastically, "Sup'n wrong with your eyesight, boy? Or did you just forget to mention they was white?"

Black men and women of all ages were staring at the Bloomfields with stony expressions, plainly not too thrilled to have a white lady and her kids in their backwoods hangout. I saw Nathan talking and gesturing earnestly to a big curvy woman I guessed was Peaches. She sauntered over, looking perfectly serene. "Hi, honey," she said to Grace. "Nathan says you need a place for the night. Sit yourselves right down and I'll send someone to get you some food."

The customers blinked at this. I could see them think, well, if Peaches thinks it's okay . . . And gradually everyone forgot about the white strangers and got on with having a good time.

Someone appeared with food, and Grace and the children gratefully tucked into pork and greens and cornbread.

Peaches was telling her customers about two prohibition agents, Izzy and Mo, who traveled around America trying to catch anyone breaking the law by making or selling illicit alcohol.

"There's nothing those devils won't do to get

their man!" She chuckled. "They'll dress up in stupid disguises. Play mean tricks. You know one of them actually stood out in the snow until he was blue with cold this one time? His partner dragged him into a bar and begged them to give him some brandy to revive him. The poor fool brought it, and you know what Izzy says then? 'Dere's saaad news!'"

"Why'd he say that?" asked someone in a puzzled voice.

"Mo and Izzy always say that, when they bust someone," she explained, laughing. "I told you, those guys are devils!"

Clem gave a drowsy giggle. "Dere's saaad news," he repeated. Minutes later he was asleep on Grace's lap.

Someone started to play a guitar in a style and rhythm I have never ever heard before and an old man began to sing in a cracked, growly voice. I can't explain why, but it was beautiful. It was raw and filled with human pain. But it wasn't like the singer was just bellyaching about his own personal troubles. He was singing for every human on Earth who'd ever suffered.

I found myself picturing all the faces I'd seen since I'd been in America: Cissie baking cookies with Clem, Grace watching her children's sleeping faces the night their father died, the yearning eyes of the woman in the hobo town by the railway tracks, and old Isaac rocking in his chair.

I saw Honesty watching intently. There was a new softness in her face and I knew that for just a moment, the pain and longing in the old blues singer's voice had reached her too.

It was past midnight when the last customer left. Peaches gave the family some clean flour sacks for blankets, then she and Nathan went home. Grace and her girls put their sacks on the floor and were fast asleep in minutes. And I thought, how come an illegal speakeasy in the middle of the woods feels so safe and peaceful?

We made good progress over the next few days, traveling up through Alabama and Mississippi and into Arkansas. The Angel Academy began to seem like a far-off dream. I occasionally wondered what Lollie and Reuben were getting up to, but only in a detached sort of way. Sometimes I felt as if I'd been traveling across the United States of America forever.

One morning a farmer dropped us off at a town called Freshwater. Grace and her children went into the drugstore to buy breakfast. And standing at the counter, buying about a zillion cups of coffee, was Lenny!

The Bloomfields had a highly emotional reunion. Even Honesty gave her brother a wintry little hug.

"So have you gone into the coffee business?" Rose teased.

But Lenny proudly insisted he was in the movie business now. "I might be fetching and carrying at present, but eventually it will lead to bigger things. Come with me and I'll introduce you to the crew."

We found the film people in their truck, waiting morosely for their morning caffeine fix. The director seemed to be having a major temper tantrum about their sloppy attitudes or whatever. He caught sight of us, and his expression changed so dramatically I thought he was going to have a stroke.

"Mr. Mantovani, are you okay?" Lenny faltered.

The director got out of the truck. He was gazing at Rose as if he was in some kind of trance. He held up his hands, forming an imaginary camera lens, and panned this way and that, peering at her startled face. "What's your name, doll?" he barked suddenly.

Rose looked annoyed. "Rose Bloomfield."

He shook his head, frowning. "Sounds like a firm of hick florists. Suppose we call you Rosa Bloom? Now that's classy."

"Maybe, but I'm happy with the name I've got," said Rose.

Mr. Mantovani reached out and removed Rose's little owl glasses.

"Hey!" she protested.

"I knew it!" he said triumphantly. "Under those hideous spectacles, you have the face of an angel. I promise you, with makeup and fancy clothes, you'll be sensational!"

Omigosh, I thought. Little Rose has been discovered! I looked at her with new interest, and I thought the director had a point. Honesty's sister only needed a string of beads to twirl and she could have been one of those enigmatic "It" girls I'd seen in Honesty's mum's magazines. In the Twenties, "It" meant sex appeal. Girls like Clara Bow and Louise Brooks had "It." And according to Cissie, Rudolf Valentino had "It." But having seen a picture, I personally prefer my heartthrobs *without* eyeliner.

I could see Rose felt totally naked without her spectacles. She grabbed them back. "What's he talking about?" she asked.

Lenny looked envious. "I think he wants to put you in his movie."

Rose gave a nervous laugh, realized Lenny was serious, and turned as pink as a tulip.

Mr. Mantovani acted offended. "Girls would kill for this opportunity, doll. I'm asking you to be my new leading lady."

"Oh thanks a bunch," said a girl in film makeup. "What am I now? Chopped liver?"

"You're a very nice girl, Ingrid," Mr. Mantovani said patronizingly. "But Rosa here is the mysterious beauty I've been searching for my whole life."

It went on like that for ages, with Rose insisting she wasn't interested, and Mr. Mantovani totally refusing to take no for an answer.

Suddenly Rose said, "How much do you pay?"

"Ha!" snorted the former leading lady.

Mr. Mantovani looked shifty. "Doll, what is money, compared with the birth of a new art form?"

"Then forget it," said Rose firmly. "I need to get my family to San Francisco."

The director frowned. "I can't give you the money, doll," he admitted. "But I could definitely get you to California."

She briskly extended her hand. "It's a deal."

I was *so* proud of her. Acting and filmmaking were completely not Rose's thing, yet she had decided to go with the flow just to help her family.

Mr. Mantovani's style people gave Honesty's sister a radical makeover. They took away her tiny owl spectacles and cut her long hair into a swingy, mischievous-looking bob. They plucked her bushy eyebrows until she was left with just two startled little crescents. The makeup artist painted Rose's sharp clever little face with Twenties-style film makeup, which instantly made her look very mysterious and geisha-like. Finally the dresser buttoned her into a low-waisted Charleston dress with exquisite beading on the hem.

When they finally let Rose see herself in the mirror, she gasped and I felt genuinely moved. I had seen about a zillion TV makeover shows in my time but I've never seen such a miraculous transformation. Rose Bloomfield had totally vanished, and in her place was Rosa Bloom, a smolderingly sexy movie star!

Boy, Melanie, I told myself, the Agency certainly moves in mysterious ways. In my scenario it was Honesty who got talent-spotted. Never in a million years did I think it would be geeky little Rose!

Clem got a part too. He played the cute curly kid with the puppy. Honesty could have been in the film if she played her cards right, but she was in full zombie mode, which didn't exactly make the film people warm to her, and eventually they left her well alone.

Can you believe it only took a week to make Mr. Mantovani's film! Actually, compared with filmmaking in my time, the process seemed really amateurish. Movies were silent then, so the actors just did loads of cheesy miming and face-pulling. To be honest, Rose didn't have that much to do in *Dangerous Pearls* (that was the name of Mr. Mantovani's movie), except look scared and pretty while the hero rescued her and her precious pearls from a string of evil villains. I know, I know, it wasn't much of a plot, but like Mr. Mantovani said, the film industry was in its infancy.

I have to admit to a bad moment when they

tied Rose to the train tracks. Okay, it wasn't so dangerous as it sounds. Lenny was crouching just out of shot, with a pen knife ready to cut her free, in case an express train suddenly came roaring out of the tunnel. But to be on the safe side, I crouched beside the rails too and surrounded Rose with protective angel vibes.

A funny sound made me look up and I saw that Honesty was trembling uncontrollably. I realized that she was totally convinced her sister was going to be horribly mashed by a train. She started moaning, "Cut her free. Quick, quick! Cut her free!"

Deep down I'd known that sneery zombie girl wasn't *my* Honesty. That's why I'd sat up with her night after night beaming vibes, trying to reach her. But now for the first time I glimpsed the terrible vulnerability she'd been trying so desperately to hide, and it shocked me right to the core.

On the last day of filming, Mr. Mantovani held a party at the town's only hotel. Officially everyone was drinking fruit punch, but I glimpsed the inevitable brown paper bag doing the rounds and everyone started getting a bit flirty and giggly. I'd noticed that banning alcohol seemed to have made it more thrilling and desirable than ever.

Just as things were getting a teensy bit out of hand, a tow truck pulled up outside. A guy in dungarees came in and peered around the crowded bar. "Is there a lady called Rosa Bloom here?"

Rose turned in surprise and her short shiny hair swooshed across her rouged cheekbones. "I guess that must be me!" She laughed.

"Sign here please and print your name clearly underneath," he said. "Oops, nearly forgot to give you the keys!"

Rose pulled a comical face at the other Bloomfields like, "What is going on?"

They all followed him outside, totally bemused. The delivery man unhitched a battered old pickup from his vehicle. "Okey dokey, she's all yours!" he said cheerily and climbed back into his cab.

Rose stared at the pickup with a stunned expression. Mr. Mantovani came up behind her. "Don't look so surprised, doll." He chuckled. "You kept your side of the deal, now I've kept mine!"

"I thought you were going to give us the train tickets," she said wonderingly. "Not our very own truck." She looked doubtful suddenly. "It isn't stolen, is it?"

"Don't insult me, Rosa! I called in some favors is all."

To everyone's surprise, Rose kissed him on both cheeks. "Why thank you, Mr. Mantovani," she said. Then she yelled, "Honesty, Clem, Mama—grab your bags, let's go!"

Lenny was looking down in the mouth. "But you can't even drive," he said.

Rose's eyes sparkled. "No, but you can, Len! Hollywood is in California too, you know. What better place to be a stuntman than Hollywood?"

Yess! I thought. Hollywood was only just starting to be known for making films in Lenny's time, so he'd be arriving at exactly the right time.

"And when all those other directors come knocking on your door, doll, tell them Tony Mantovani saw you first!" the director called plaintively.

Rose laughed. "I told you, I'm not interested in movies. When we get to California I'm going to college and one day I'll be a famous archaeologist."

She climbed into the back of the old pickup, put her glasses on, and started to read. I had to smile. With her new confidence and "It" girl haircut, Honesty's bookworm sister looked gorgeous, even in her hideous specs.

Lenny, Grace, and Clem climbed into the front of the truck. Lenny started singing, "California here I come!" and Grace and Clem joined in.

I suddenly felt desperately sad vibes coming from somewhere close by. Honesty had seated herself as far away from Rose as humanly possible. She had her usual grim zombie expression, but for the first time in weeks, I heard her thoughts.

Everyone is following their dreams. Everyone but me.

I had a terrifying insight. It wasn't that Honesty didn't have a dream. She did. A totally impossible one. She wanted everything the way it was before her father died. She wanted to be living with her mama and papa in suburban Philadelphia, scoring As and Bs at school. And if she couldn't have that, she didn't want anything. In other words, she was going to stay a zombie for the rest of her life.

I experienced the sickening sensation I get when I'm seriously out of my depth.

Admit it, Melanie, you are a hopeless guardian angel, I told myself unhappily. You have beamed so many vibes at this poor girl, she ought to glow in the dark by now. But not only is she not getting better. She's actually getting *worse*. You've got to hand her over to the professionals, before it's too late.

I called up the GA hotline as we bumped along in the back of the truck. It was hard to talk, partly because of the truck, partly because I was trying not to cry, and also because bits of my hair kept blowing into my mouth.

"Orlando," I sniveled. "You'd better tell the Agency to send someone else. I'm just not getting through to her."

"You are," he insisted. "You being there is helping her more than you know."

"I just don't understand her," I wailed. "To be honest, I don't even like her that much." It was the first time I'd admitted this even to myself, and I felt a rush of shame. What kind of guardian angel *dislikes* her human?

As usual, Orlando was serenely unshockable. "Give her time. Honesty hasn't come to terms with her father's death, that's all."

"Come to terms!" I wailed. "Orlando, she hasn't shed a single tear!"

"Of course not. She's completely frozen inside. That's how the PODS like it."

I felt myself turn cold. "Omigosh!" I gasped. "The PODS got to her when I wasn't looking!" I'd got so used to the dark powers operating on a huge scale—world wars, famines, famous authors, and whatever—I had stupidly forgotten that ordinary individuals were equally at risk.

"I don't think they targeted her deliberately," Orlando was saying. "But it's easy for someone as vulnerable as Honesty to tune into a PODS wavelength. Now she's getting blasted with toxic vibes twenty-four hours a day."

I had also stupidly forgotten that we're not the only cosmic beings who broadcast vibes. I am *so* useless, I thought.

As usual, Orlando read my mind. "Don't beat yourself up, Melanie," he said calmly. "Honesty Bloomfield called *you*, remember?" And he hung up.

But I knew I had failed her just when she needed me most, and I was disgusted with myself.

I was crying seriously by this time, and I'd got to the crucial stage when you need a really good blow. I scrabbled in my bag on the off-chance I'd brought some tissues and was astonished to find a bulky paperback.

How weird, I thought. I completely didn't remember packing my Angel Handbook. It must have fallen in when I wasn't looking. Then I whispered, "Omigosh, it's a sign!"

I shut my eyes tight, then quickly opened the Angel Handbook at random and read, "It is said that it is better to travel hopefully than to arrive."

I looked up and saw Honesty staring emptily into space as if she had no idea where she was going and couldn't care less if she arrived. And I remembered her singing the nickelodeon song, and suddenly I felt this ache inside my heart.

Orlando's right, I thought. She called me and I mustn't let her down.

Chapter Seven

ALL THROUGH TEXAS AND into Oklahoma, I stuck to Honesty like glue.

I didn't just beam vibes, I chatted to her non-stop. I even sang to her. I figured, if it works with coma victims, it could work with Honesty too. Assuming Orlando was right, her fragile energy system was getting a twenty-four-hour battering from PODS FM. Our vibes are designed to make humans feel stronger, so they can get on with whatever they came to Earth to do. But the vibes the PODS put out literally poison human minds and hearts, making their lives seem totally meaningless.

Humans have free will as you know, so I couldn't disconnect Honesty from the PODS, even if I knew how. She had to do that herself. My job as Honesty's guardian angel was to remind her there were other cosmic vibes available: uplifting, inspiring, groovy, feel-good vibes.

We sat in the back of the pickup, rattling across huge empty prairies under an equally huge empty sky. Oklahoma weather is really something else. One minute we'd be driving along in a blizzard, the next we'd be basking in hot sunlight. In one place we ran into the tail end of one of those midwestern twisters (that's like a cyclone). To everyone's horror, it started raining frogs! Rose and Honesty shrieked and threw the icky things out as fast as they landed. But I totally refused to let a local frog storm distract me from my mission. And when I was quite sure frogs had stopped falling out of the sky, I settled down beside Honesty, and told her the story of my own short, sweet but incredibly cool life on Earth. Oh, and I set her straight about that cloud-filled waiting room, in case she was worrying.

"Heaven won't be the same for your papa as it is for me, obviously," I explained. "For one thing, I was only thirteen when I died. But if he has half the fun me and Lollie have, I promise he'll be having a ball!"

I also apologized to Honesty for dissing her the way I did, when she turned out to be just a regular person instead of some precocious child star.

"You're really special, Honesty," I told her. "And you have your own special path to follow. But your dad's death really shocked you and the PODS took advantage. I am your guardian angel and I'm going to help you through this, okay?"

One afternoon the Bloomfields picked up a Mexican woman with a baby. The woman had obviously been walking for hours, and was completely exhausted. Rose immediately put down her book and took the baby, so his mother could sleep in the back of the truck. He started grizzling and she hushed him in her arms, and started to sing a Twenties ballad about true love and apple blossom, only she made it sound like a lullaby. She had a surprisingly tuneful voice.

I was completely charmed. It was the first time I'd seen this side of Rose. Honesty was watching her too. She had this new alert expression in her eyes, almost as if she was making mental notes.

Since they'd left Georgia, Honesty's family had been living a hand-to-mouth existence. But I happened to know that Grace wasn't completely penniless. She still had a valuable diamond ring that her husband had given her. She kept it wrapped inside a blue silk scarf inside a secret pocket inside what Americans call a purse, and I call a handbag. Once I saw Grace take it out when her children were asleep, and touch it to her cheek. I didn't blame her for not wanting to part with it. The ring was the only thing she had left of her husband.

Sometimes Lenny managed to earn a few dollars, helping out at farms or country homesteads along the way. But they often went to sleep hungry, and most nights they slept under the stars.

The Bloomfield kids were scarcely recognizable as the same people who had left Philadelphia. They looked browner and wirier and somehow tougher, even little Clem. And their Philadelphia clothes were starting to get faded and raggedy around the edges. It wasn't easy to keep clean on the road, and any time the Bloomfields came to a public washroom, they dived inside and made the most of the free soap and hot water. I could only look on with envy. That's one big drawback to being a celestial agent. We can't use earthly facilities. Our molecules are too subtle or something. For the same reason, we can't tuck into the local cuisine. We have to make do with a kind of angelic trail mix, which luckily is quite sustaining.

Despite the tough conditions, Honesty's mother still managed to keep herself looking good. Grace Bloomfield struck me as one of those natural celebrities. She wasn't snooty or superior, yet she had this real air about her. Our fellow travelers noticed it and treated her with respect.

And we met all kinds on the road, I can tell you. Nineteen twenties America was positively heaving with colorful characters with weird Twenties-type occupations. As you probably guessed, quite a few of the occupations had to do with booze. Rum-runners smuggled it across the state line, bootleggers sold it, and moonshiners were the people who manufactured the stuff. But there were also holy rollers, preaching hellfire and damnation to anyone who would listen, quack doctors selling miracle cures for every known ailment (yeah, right!), and flashy salesmen hoping to make a quick buck. We also ran into a smooth-talking land speculator. This conman was trying to dupe people into buying "building land" in Florida. But Lenny said it was probably pure swamp.

One evening Lenny stopped the truck to give a lift to a man called Caleb Jones. He said he was heading west hoping to find work as a fruit picker. It was getting late so Grace invited him to share their supper. "That's if you don't mind bean and potato stew," she said apologetically.

"Sounds like a regular feast to me," he said.

They all sat by the campfire, eating stew and listening to the howling of a pack of nearby prairie wolves.

"Couldn't help noticing your truck seems to be developing a problem with its exhaust," he said shyly. "I'll fix it for you, if you'll let me."

As Grace said later, Caleb was a guy you could pass in a crowd without noticing. He wasn't tall or good-looking or exceptionally ugly. Yet he gave off this completely peaceful vibe, which is something you rarely find in humans.

I heard him talking to Grace when the others were asleep. "Your younger daughter seems troubled," he said. "Was she always that way?"

Grace shook her head. "Just since her daddy died."

He nodded as if he'd suspected something of the kind.

"I've been telling myself she'll come out of it," Grace said. "But lately I've been thinking, what if Honesty just goes deeper and deeper into herself and never comes out?"

I felt my skin prickle with sympathy. But I noticed that Caleb didn't immediately try to make Grace feel better. He just sat there, turning over what she had said, and for a few minutes there was no sound except the crackling of the fire and the familiar night sounds of the prairie.

Then he said quietly, "Sometimes I think the strongest people in this world are those who go down into the dark and come out the other side."

"Are you talking from experience, Mr. Jones?" Grace asked him.

"Fifteen years in Singsing," he said calmly, "and a whole bunch of other penal institutions before that. But hell, I was a prisoner long before they put me away. In here." He tapped his head.

I saw Grace register that she was alone in the dark with a violent criminal. Then she took a good look at Caleb's peaceful face, and seemed to relax. "But you got out—of both prisons?"

The man gave her an extraordinarily sweet smile. "Once you're free inside, ain't a thing in this world anyone can do to you."

Caleb Jones went on his way at first light, while the family was still sleeping. I saw him go to the truck and fix its damaged exhaust with some wire and a piece of old bandage. Then he picked some yellow wiry-stemmed flowers, some kind of prairie daisy, and left them where Grace would see them as soon as she woke up.

Rose was horrified when she heard about their midnight conversation. "He could have murdered us in our beds, Mama!"

But Grace said, "I don't care what he used to be, Rose. It's who he is now that counts. And the man I talked to last night is one of the finest gentlemen I have ever met."

Oklahoma had been gradually morphing into New Mexico, a dreamlike world of mystical mountains, tumbled red rocks, and weird flowering cacti. Pink adobe houses nestled on slopes, and goats, pigs, and chickens wandered about outside.

I felt as if we'd strayed into a totally foreign country. On the road, we passed dark-eyed men and women in vividly colored woolen clothes, struggling under loads of avocados, knobbly chili peppers, or limes. The people called out to the Bloomfields and their voices made me briefly homesick for Lola. I wondered where she was and what kind of human she was looking after. Wherever she was, I really hoped my soul mate was having fun.

Soon after midday, Lenny stopped at a gas station. An absolutely ancient guy in dungarees came out to fill up the truck. "Where you headed?" he asked.

"California," said Lenny.

The garage guy pointed to a figure slumped beside the petrol pumps, apparently sound asleep. "Got a feller here needs to get to Santa Fe."

"We're going over that way," said Lenny.

The old man gave a piercing whistle. "Gideon, you got yourself a ride!"

The man tipped back his cowboy hat, yawning. When he saw the Bloomfields, his face split into a lazy grin and he got to his feet. "Well, thank you kindly!"

I think it was Gideon's eyes that made me feel uneasy. They seemed to be everywhere at once, flickering over faces, purses, and pockets as if he had some spooky X-ray vision. He acted so sleepy and benign, yet I found his vibes totally chilling. I suspected that Gideon was one of those humans who had come a *leetle* bit too close to the PODS for comfort. I tried to tune in to his thoughts, but it wasn't like tuning in to a normal adult human. Gideon was more like some hyperactive little kid, constantly going "gimme

gimme gimme." I could tell the Bloomfields didn't like him either, but they generously took him all the way to Santa Fe.

That night the family set up camp. Clem wandered around collecting firewood, which was his special chore. After a few minutes, he came trailing back and drooped against Grace. "Mama, I don't feel so good."

She felt his forehead and looked dismayed. "Oh, my stars!" she murmured. "The child's burning up!" I saw her frantically thinking what to do. "Lenny, I know you've been driving all day, but we've got to find this little boy a doctor."

Everyone piled back into the truck and Lenny drove for another two hours in pitch darkness, on a narrow road with hair-raising bends. Clem had started muttering nonsense to himself. Grace stayed calm but I could feel Honesty silently freaking out.

We came to a small town called Sweet Rock, perched on a rocky hillside above the river. The Bloomfields checked into a Spanish-style inn called *The Laughing Horse* and Grace asked them to call a doctor.

They went up to their rooms and Grace undressed a weak trembling Clem. She lifted her little boy onto the bed and I saw his eyes roll right up into his head.

Honesty looked scared. "What's wrong with him, Mama?" she said in a small voice.

"He's just delirious," said Grace. "Could you fetch me a bowl of water, Rose? I'll sponge him down while we're waiting for the doctor."

"How are we going to pay for all of this, Mama?" Rose said anxiously. "Hotels and doctors cost money."

Grace tried to smile. "It's all right, I still have your daddy's ring." She reached into her bag and pulled out the blue silk scarf. She unwrapped it tenderly, then stared in horror at the dirty pebble inside.

"I am so stupid," she said in a harsh voice. "I knew Gideon was a phoney and I let him go right ahead and make a fool of me."

"You think Gideon stole your ring?" said Lenny incredulously.

"There is not a doubt in my mind."

Grace crouched down beside her open suitcase and started hunting for something.

"Clem is going to die, isn't he!" Honesty was chalk-white and trembling.

Grace stopped her rummaging. She took hold

of Honesty and forced her to look into her eyes. "No, Clem is not going to die. He's got a high fever, that's all. Once it goes down, he'll be better in no time."

Grace went back to her seach. Suddenly she gave a sigh of relief. "He didn't get this at least." She held up the check her father had written all those weeks ago in Georgia.

"The Lord surely works in mysterious ways," she said gratefully. "I never did understand why I didn't just tear up that old buzzard's money. But I am truly glad I didn't."

The doctor came and clicked his tongue at Clem's condition. "Your son is exhausted and badly dehydrated. He needs fluids, bed rest, and most of all, a calm, stable environment," he told Grace as he wrote out a prescription.

After he'd gone, she paced up and down the room, looking totally haunted. "Why didn't he just come out and say, 'You are a terrible mother, Grace Bloomfield. You made your little boy ill by dragging him selfishly all over America'?" she said despairingly.

Grace was unnaturally quiet all the rest of the evening. I wanted to read her thoughts, but didn't feel as if I should intrude on her privacy. I could tell she was trying to work out what to do for the best.

Next morning she announced that they were staying put in Sweet Rock, until Clem had recovered. I thought Grace's instincts were totally sound, and decided to do everything I could to back her up. Angels aren't supposed to interfere with human destinies, but as you know, there are times when a teeny cosmic nudge can make all the difference. I dialed up the GA hotline and asked Orlando for help.

"Hi, it's Mel! Sorry to hassle you, but the Bloomfields need to crash for a while," I rattled off breathlessly. "Do you think the Agency could find them somewhere to rent around here? Plus it would be helpful if Lenny could get work locally. The way I look at it, we're just helping them to help themselves, right?"

"I'll see if I can pull a few strings," he promised.

I never found out what cosmic strings Orlando pulled, if any, but the Agency definitely delivered the goods. The very first time Rose and Lenny went house-hunting, they found the coolest little cottage to let on the edge of town. It was built out of rose-colored adobe, a kind of local mud, and it looked exactly like those houses in Luke Skywalker's hometown in the *Star Wars* movie. Rose and Honesty set to work making it homey, leaving Grace free to look after Clem. And the day after they moved in, Lenny found work on a neighboring ranch.

I can't explain why New Mexico felt so right. Maybe it was all those angel place names: Angel Point, Angel Canyon, Angel Fire. But I was absolutely certain this was the perfect place for Clem to grow strong and well again after all his weeks on the road.

And guess what! It turned out to be perfect for Lenny's love life too!

Clem was getting better by this time, so when the circus arrived in Sweet Rock Lenny took the girls along for a treat. Naturally I tagged along. We filed into the tent and squeezed ourselves on to one of the front benches overlooking the circus ring. The locals were merrily turning their circus outing into a major fiesta. Children threw colored streamers and tooted horns. Mothers kept handing Lenny and the girls delicious New Mexican goodies. Old grannies pinched Lenny's cheek and told him how handsome he was. And the grandpas insisted on giving him swigs of the local hooch which, being macho New Mexicans, they didn't even bother to hide.

Once again I saw that alert little gleam in Honesty's eyes as if she was amused despite herself.

It wasn't the most sophisticated circus: a couple of clowns, some brave geriatric elephants, and a wobbly trapeze artist in grubby pink tights. Then the ring master bawled, "Presenting the one and only, magnificent Ruby Rio!" and I felt that prickle of angel electricity that means something is going to happen.

A golden-skinned girl rode into the ring on a palomino pony. She had flashing dark eyes and her glittery scarlet costume left little to the imagination. The pony began to trot faster, and suddenly Ruby Rio stood upright on the pony's bare back. She gave a whoop of triumph and struck what had to be the sassiest pose the people of Sweet Rock had ever seen.

Without warning, she let herself fall backward. But just as it seemed she was sure to hit the sawdust, she casually reached out to save herself, and continued to ride round the ring, *underneath* the pony!

There was a collective gasp and Lenny's tortilla fell from his hand. Omigosh, I thought. The girl is pure dynamite! Plus her dress sense is totally slamming! Honesty was obviously mesmerized. So was Rose.

Ruby and her pony clearly had some telepathic link, because no matter how high she leaped, or how many times she spun around in the air, or how far she slid under its belly, Ruby effortlessly got back onto her horse. She even rode around the ring standing on her head. The audience went mad, clapping and stamping and yelling out in Spanish. The atmosphere was electric!

When the show was over, Lenny said huskily, "You girls go home."

"Why, where are you going?" asked Rose. For someone so clever, she could be really dense sometimes. Hadn't she heard of love at first sight?

Ruby Rio turned out to be half Native American and half New Mexican cowgirl, so you could say she was always destined to be out of the ordinary. But what I think is so sweet is that this incredible girl had spotted Lenny in the audience, and instantly fell in love with *him* at first sight too! Can you believe that she and Lenny even shared the exact same dream of going to Hollywood as famous stunt persons?

So when the doctor gave Clem the all-clear at last and the family was able to continue on their journey, Ruby Rio came too, bringing her impressive collection of costumes.

"Next stop Arizona!" Lenny said happily, putting the truck into gear. "In a couple of days we'll be in the City of the Angels!"

Oh yeah, I thought. Duh! I'd never actually registered the true meaning of Los Angeles before.

I have to admit that as we got closer I was getting totally overexcited. I was like, I can't *believe* I'm going to be in Hollywood at the dawn of moving pictures. I might see Charlie Chaplin or Laurel and Hardy, or my own personal favorite, Harold Lloyd—stars that were, like, *legends*.

It's a pity no one was filming our arrival in Hollywood, because as we chugged into Sunset Boulevard, Mr. Mantovani's faithful truck spluttered, choked, and died spectacularly. The truck obviously wasn't going anywhere, so everyone got out.

I immediately ran up to the Sunset Boulevard sign, going, "Woo, we're in Hollywood! Oh, wow, this is so cool!" I was fizzing with happiness.

Lenny whispered to Ruby, "I'll make you proud

of me, you'll see."

I saw Honesty shiver in the California sun. She wrapped her arms around herself, scowling. "None of this is real," she said. "Not a single thing. They imported the palm trees from Hawaii. It's all totally fake."

I knew this wasn't Honesty talking. It was just Honesty under the influence of PODS FM. She felt lost and scared and she didn't even know why.

She's going to need my input more than ever, I thought. Being on the road is one thing. Now she's got to make a new life in completely strange surroundings.

My mobile rang. Yippee! I thought, I can swank to Orlando about being in Hollywood. "You'll never guess where I am—" I babbled.

"I know exactly where you are," he said. "And now it's time to come back."

All my fizzy happiness drained out of my feet. "But I'm just getting the hang of being a guardian angel!" I wailed.

"I know, and everyone thinks you're doing fine, but it's time you had a break."

"I don't want a break!" I fumed. "It totally doesn't make sense for me to leave Honesty now."

Orlando sounded annoyingly serene. "I know

it seems that way," he agreed. "But the Agency is generally good on cosmic timing."

"Cosmic baloney!" I raged. "They send me to look after this damaged girl, then just when she needs me the most, they tell you to pull me out!" I was practically yelling into my mobile. "I *know* Honesty, okay? And she's still really vulnerable! You've got to let me stay!"

And I only just got to Hollywood, I screamed silently.

"Sorry Mel, rules are rules," said Orlando. "Don't worry. They'll have her on twenty-four-hour Angel Watch."

And before I had a chance to say good-bye, a beam of light came down and I went blasting back to Heaven.

Chapter Eight

MY HOMECOMING FELT completely unreal. I sat in the limo, watching familiar landmarks flow by in the velvety dusk, and breathing the celestial air with its haunting scent that is almost, but not quite, like lilacs. But I wasn't really here.

I kept seeing Honesty in the middle of Sunset Boulevard, shivering in the California sunshine and dissing everything in sight.

Back at the dorm I found a note on my door.

Wake me the instant you get in,
Big Love
Lollie xxx

I hadn't let myself miss my soul mate too much while I'd been gone. It would have been way too painful. But I was now totally desperate to see her.

I badly needed a shower and change of clothes, but I couldn't possibly wait that long, so I immediately banged on her door. There was a long pause. Eventually this mad curly bed-head poked out.

"Ta da!" I said.

"Omigosh, Boo!" she shrieked. "It feels like a lifetime!"

We jumped up and down, hugging each other and squealing excitedly.

Lola said, "I'm going to give you two options, *carita*. Option A, you catch up on your beauty sleep like a good sensible angel, or Option B, you, me, and Sweetpea hit the Babylon right away and you do the beauty sleep thing later. What do you say?"

I slapped her palm. "Option B for Babylon! I'm beautiful enough already."

Lola sniffed the air. "Beautiful yes, but also strangely stinky."

"I've been hanging out with hoodlums and hobos," I said. "What do you expect?"

"Ooh," said Lola. "Tell me more." She followed

me into my room and we yelled scraps of news to each other as I showered.

Over the sound of rushing water, Lola told me about the tribal princess she'd been minding in ancient Persia or wherever. "Her tribe breeds herds of fabulous horses and they travel with them from place to place. When they're not killing people from other tribes, the men are really spiritual and romantic. They give their sweethearts roses and recite Persian love poetry. The women are as fierce as the men," she explained. "They all ride like demons, even tiny kids."

"I met a girl who can ride like a demon too," I yelled, thinking of Ruby Rio.

"Is she your human, Boo?"

"Uh-uh. Erm, actually my human is kind of complicated," I said lamely. I found that I totally didn't know how to put my 1920s experiences into words. I put on my fluffy robe and blow-dried my hair, and I didn't say another word about Honesty. Probably Lola guessed how I felt, because she flung open my wardrobe door and said cheerfully, "Okay, girlfriend, what are you going to wear?"

I threw on some jeans, a T-shirt that said *Little*

Miss Naughty (when in doubt go for the classics!), splashed on some Attitude, my fave heavenly fragrance, and I was ready to go.

Lola and I headed down to the Babylon Café, arm in arm.

We found Reuben at our favorite outdoor table. I thought my buddy looked unusually tense. I reckoned his Earth experiences might have been a shock to his system, so I said sympathetically, "Was it really tough?"

"Actually it was great," he said. "I'm looking after this little cabin boy who got mixed up in the Napoleonic wars. Erm, Mel, before I get into that, I've got something to tell you."

I was trying to figure out which delicious fruit punch to have. The Babylon does about a zillion varieties. "Yeah," I said vaguely. "What?"

"Orlando thought you'd rather hear it from me."

Reuben sounded so worried that I looked up.

"Brice is back," he said.

I put down my menu. I was so shocked, I could hardly get the words out. "Back here? No way!"

"Yes way," said Reuben. "He's practically the first person I saw when I got back to school."

"They let him back into our school?"

Reuben nodded unhappily. "I knew you'd be upset."

"I'm not upset, okay! I'm shocked, I'm sick to my stomach, I'm, I'm . . ."

"Upset," Lola supplied helpfully.

All my feelings burst out in a rush. "It's outrageous! Brice can't just waltz back and call himself an angel after the things he's done. After the things he did to you, Reuben!" I reminded him angrily. "Okay, so we saw a different side to him when we met him in the future. And okay, so he's not one hundred percent evil, but that hardly qualifies him to be an angel!"

I saw Reuben absently fingering his scar under his tunic, a souvenir of the savage beating Brice gave him in Tudor times. The Sanctuary angels could have healed it totally, but Reuben insisted on keeping it. He said he wanted to show all his mates that he was hard. But I think it was really a reminder to stay focused. You know, an angel warrior kind of thing.

I was still waiting for my friends to show me some sympathy, but there was just a long awkward silence.

Then Lola said, "Who knows, maybe Brice has

changed? Maybe he's gone through his evil PODS phase and come out the other side, and from now on he'll be an absolutely incredible celestial agent."

"Oh *please,*" I said. "Are you one of his little groupies now or something?"

She looked hurt. "Hey, Boo, I'm your best friend, but don't push your luck."

"Let's not talk about this now," said Reuben quickly. "We've only got a couple of days off. Let's just have fun, okay?"

It's all right for them, I thought. Brice hadn't been their cosmic stalker. They had no idea how insecure it made me feel, knowing I might walk into one of my favorite heavenly haunts and find my worst nightmares looking back at me.

When I finally climbed into my economy-sized bed, I was still freaking out inside. I didn't have the most restful night, I have to say. I kept dreaming I was back on Earth. I saw Ruby hanging up her costumes in the new apartment, and Lenny came in and gave her a kiss. Honesty was at the window staring down into a sunny courtyard, and I got the weirdest feeling she was missing me. I tried to tell her I was coming back, but the instant I heard my own voice, I woke up.

I must have been doing some unusually hard thinking in my sleep, because I didn't feel nearly as anti-Brice as I had the night before.

You're such a hypocrite, Mel Beeby, I scolded myself. You don't go riding in on your high horse every time a human makes a mistake. That Caleb Jones must have been into some heavy stuff to get put in Singsing, but he came out of it, and now he's this streetwise guru.

I found myself remembering what Michael said. That we couldn't be effective guardian angels, unless we were, like, *flawed* and understood human suffering. Well, Brice was flawed all right and he'd suffered for it in ways I'd probably never know.

Maybe one day Brice would evolve into a streetwise guru angel. Maybe not. Either way, it was his and the Agency's business, not mine.

I was just getting dressed, when Lola came to find me. We decided to pick up some picnic goodies from Guru and spend the day on the beach, getting our strength back for phase two of our GA assignments.

We lay on sparkling white sand in our bikinis, soaking up the rays, and listening to the soft hush hush of the heavenly waves.

Suddenly Lola said, "I love being a guardian angel, but have you noticed how you're never off duty, even now when you're back home?"

"Even when you're asleep!" I said ruefully.

She sat up. "Did you dream about yours too?"

"Only all night long! Actually I'm kind of missing mine."

"Me too," Lola admitted. "It's weird. I didn't even like her at first!"

"Ditto." I giggled.

See what I mean? Lola and I are total soul mates. We can say anything to each other, and the other person will understand.

Her expression changed, and she reached out and patted my hand. "Michael would never have let him come back, if it wasn't right," she said softly.

She didn't have to say who she meant.

"I know," I said. "I'm trying to be more mature, babe. That's what the angel business is all about, right? Evolution. Trees and diamonds and whatever."

By the time I got back to school, I was totally at one with the cosmos. Orlando was right, I thought. I had needed a break. But now I was going back and I was going to be the best GA

Hollywood has ever seen!

I was figuring out what to pack, when the phone rang beside my bed. It was Michael. "Sorry, I should have called, but I've been tied up."

"I know, don't say it. My old century." I sighed.

"Could be," he said humorously. "But I'm here now. And in your opinion, how is Honesty doing?"

I took a breath. "In my opinion? Not great. Orlando thinks she accidentally tuned into a PODS wavelength. She's totally withdrawn inside herself and I don't think just sending vibes is going to bring her out."

There was a pause. Then Michael said, "I think you'd better come down and pick out a suitable outfit, Ms. Beeby."

I gasped. "You are kidding! You don't mean . . . ?"

"You're saying that Honesty needs a friend. I happen to agree with you, which is why I'm giving you official permission to materialize."

Chapter Nine

I'D ONLY MATERIALIZED TWICE BEFORE. The first time I stupidly did it without permission, and almost got myself chucked out of the Academy. The second time I even more stupidly dived through a wormhole into the future and materialized by pure accident.

Now for the first time I was materializing with the Agency's blessing, which is practically unheard of for a trainee.

The Agency style adviser showed me and Michael all the delicious clothes I had to choose from, and I got totally overexcited. We picked out two authentically aged outfits, one to wear and one to pack in my real 1920s suitcase. After that I had to choose chemises and stockings and whatever. I think it was the underwear that suddenly made it seem real.

"Michael, I don't think this is going to work,"

I said, panicking. "As far as the Bloomfields are concerned, I'm a stranger. I can't just, like, move in with them."

"We've been doing this for quite a while, you know," Michael assured me. "I think you'll find it will all work out."

But when I stepped onto planet Earth a couple of hours later, my knees felt weak with stage fright. Can you believe I found myself outside the exact same Spanish-style apartment building I'd seen in my dream? I could hear a dance tune playing on a crackly radio: "Not much money, oh but honey, ain't we got fun!"

A warm breeze rattled the fronds of the palm trees. The wind was surprisingly strong. Suddenly a red feather boa came snaking through the air and wrapped itself softly around my head.

I disentangled myself and saw Ruby and Honesty running out of the building. They started picking up pieces of glitzy circus clothing. I was just about to rush up to say hi, when I remembered. *Duh!* They didn't actually know me yet!

Then quite spontaneously, Ruby said, "Could you hold this a moment?" and dumped a heap of clothes in my arms. "I was airing my costumes, and the wind blew them off the balcony." She grinned.

I took a couple of microseconds to assimilate the good news—that I was now 100 percent visible to the human race. Ohh, this is better, I thought happily, and my nerves totally melted away. I was so thrilled to be able to chat to them in visible form like this, that I spoke right from the heart. "I can't believe it! I've always dreamed of going to Hollywood, and finally I'm really here!"

I saw Ruby register my lonely little suitcase. "Got any folks?" she asked sympathetically.

I shook my head. "I guess you could say I'm kind of a free agent," I said, which wasn't exactly a lie.

"Stop with us, till you get fixed up," she said impulsively. "Your mama won't mind, will she, Honesty?"

Honesty took a faltering step toward me. I was astonished to see wondering recognition in her eyes. "Have we met before?" she said softly. "I feel like I know you from somewhere."

I suddenly felt really shy. "I don't think so," I told her. "I've probably just got one of those faces."

But inside I was going, omigosh, this is so sweet! Honesty recognized me!

I had totally new respect for angel vibes after that, I can tell you. I didn't even have to try to win Honesty's confidence. It's like she just knew she could trust me.

Honesty even said I could share her little box room, if I didn't mind nocturnal gurgles from the hot water tank. She thoughtfully emptied out two of her drawers and made some space in her closet, and while I put my things away, she told me what everyone in the family was up to these days.

Even allowing for differences in earthly and heavenly time systems, the Bloomfields had got work really speedily.

Rose was doing modeling, would you believe? (Don't panic, she kept her clothes on! It was her "It" girl face everyone went crazy about.) Grace had landed herself a magic job, playing the piano at a Hollywood movie theater called the Golden Palace Picture House. Ruby and Lenny worked in a Hollywood nightclub called the Top Hat Club. Honesty told me that the club was run by two brothers, Carlo and Luigi Franco, who owned a string of clubs all over LA.

Ruby was actually performing in the nightly cabaret. Lenny was just waiting on tables at present, but Honesty said he was sure to get his break really soon.

And guess what! Next day I got a job too! Over breakfast, Ruby offered to wangle me a few hours at the club doing washing up. Suddenly Honesty coughed and said, "What about me?" And Ruby just said, "Sure."

So four nights a week, Honesty and I washed dishes at the Top Hat. This was way more cool than it sounds because we got to see all the cabaret acts for free, including Ruby's. With Lenny's help she had worked up a v. exotic acrobatic routine, with some fire-eating thrown in for added excitement.

On the club's quieter nights, Lenny hung out with us, watching the other artists' acts. He wasn't very impressed with any of them, I have to say. But he really *really* hated the girl who played the musical saw.

"That stuff belongs back in the nineteenth century along with the—the barrel organ and horse-drawn carriages," he insisted. "Times have changed. People today need danger and daring! They need speed, novelty, and excitement. More than that, they need magic!"

Lenny's eyes went all misty. I could tell he was picturing himself and Ruby drawing oohs and aahs from the crowd with some death-defying maneuver. Lenny might have to work as a waiter, but in his mind, he was a stuntman-in-waiting. He and Ruby spent every spare moment down in the courtyard devising weird and wonderful stunts.

"I like that mad stunt you do with the bicycle," I said shyly. "That's magic. It's funny too!"

Lenny's face lit up. "You really think so? Do you think maybe we could make the big time?"

"I know so—" I began.

A voice yelled, "Lenny! Get over here. Luigi's got an urgent message that needs to be delivered."

I saw Lenny tense. "I'd better go."

"Let them wait," Honesty hissed at him. "They pay you to wait on tables, not to be Luigi's dogsbody."

I agreed with her. The Franco brothers treated Lenny like their own personal slave, constantly making him run their stupid little errands for them. They were really picky too, like Lenny had to go to this one particular florist even if it was, like, after midnight.

Lenny patted his sister's shoulder. "You're a good kid. But I know what I'm doing." He was smiling but I noticed that he couldn't quite meet her eyes.

Violet was what the Agency had decided I should be called. But like Shakespeare said, "What's in a name?" My name might be bogus, but my friendship was totally genuine. And I know it showed, because now that we were finally hanging out together, like one to one, Honesty started to come out of her shell.

They weren't so big on security back then, so in our free time we would wander into the studio lots, and roam around the empty film sets. One was a ballroom with fake marble pillars. Cissie had taught Honesty a cool little dance routine, to *Puttin' on the Ritz*. Honesty showed me the steps and we danced up and down the ballroom, singing out the lyrics.

On non-work nights, we went to the movies. The projectionist at the Golden Palace let us go up into the projection box, so we got to see all the latest films for free.

Honesty and I didn't always share the same tastes. Like, I totally didn't get the Keystone Cops and she was a big fan. But no matter what movie they were showing, I was happy to go along. I just adored that whole Twenties movie experience. I loved being up in the projectionist's room, listening to the atmospheric whirr of the projector. And I loved watching that flickering ghostly light streaming down into the dark auditorium, and miraculously transforming itself into moving pictures on the screen. But more than anything I loved the audience's excitement. When the lights dimmed and the titles came up, I could literally feel people letting go of their troubles as the movie took them away from their hard-up, humdrum lives, into another, more thrilling world.

One night we went to see a new Buster Keaton film. Grace's mother was in the auditorium playing the piano as usual. I thought she did a fantastic job. She had to keep one eye on the screen the whole time she was playing, ready to switch styles at a moment's notice. She had to play comical plonky sounds for the funny parts, mad thunderous chords for the action scenes, and heart-rending music for the sad bits.

It was really warm and cozy up in the projectionist's box. Honesty and I sat on the floor, absentmindedly stuffing our faces with popcorn, totally caught up in Buster's antics. Suddenly we heard a loud snore. The projectionist was quite old, and he'd just dozed off. Unfortunately he'd done it during the most thrilling part of the movie! There was a mad clattery unraveling sound, as the reel of film ran out. The screen went totally blank and the audience started to boo and catcall. Grace totally saved the day, luckily. She stopped playing comical Buster Keaton music, and switched to a soothing classical piece—the *Moonlight Sonata,* Honesty said it was—while the old guy frantically replaced the reel.

On the way home that night, I caught sight of two figures on the other side of the street. They were sheltering in a shadowy doorway, and one was handing over a bulky package. He looks a bit like Lenny, I thought in surprise. Then I looked again and he'd gone.

I suddenly got a really iffy vibe. "Did you see those guys over there?" I asked Honesty.

She shook her head. "Uh-uh. And if you've got any sense, you didn't either." She sounded deadly serious.

I felt a shiver run through me. "How come?"

"He was probably delivering bootleg booze.

Next time look the other way," she said solemnly, "or you could get yourself into trouble."

Honesty explained that America's prohibition laws had led to a humungous crime wave. "Gangsters like Al Capone are making millions of dollars every year, selling alcohol illegally."

"Al Capone!" I squeaked. "Al Capone lives in these times?"

She gave me a startled look. "Why, what other times would he live in?"

Yikes! I had just committed a major time booboo. I did one of my specialty airhead giggles. "I am such a ditz! My old teacher used to say I had pink fluff for brains. Sorry babe, you were telling me about the gangsters."

"The real trouble starts when they think other gangsters are muscling in on their business," Honesty explained. "After we got here, a famous LA mobster mysteriously 'disappeared.' They found him at the bottom of the river. There was some big war going on between rival gangs over who ruled which patch. The government is so worried that they employ special government agents to hunt down anyone making, buying, or selling illegal liquor."

Honesty let out this incredibly infectious giggle.

I giggled too, but out of pure shock. It was the first time I'd heard her laugh since she left Philadelphia.

"What's funny?" I asked her.

"I was remembering something I heard about these insane prohibition agents, called Izzy and Mo. They're so crazy to catch bootleggers, there's nothing they won't do. Play tricks, wear ridiculous disguises, they're like—like comic-book characters almost. And do you know what they say every time they bust someone?"

I had to bite my lip so as not to spoil her story. "No, what?"

Honesty rocked with laughter. "'Dere's saaad news!' Isn't that hilarious! 'Dere's saaad news!'"

"Sounds like a sheep!" I spluttered.

We walked along still giggling. On impulse I said, "You're so smart, Honesty."

She blinked with surprise. "How come?"

"You know all this stuff, and you take an interest in the world. You notice all the juicy little details, which pass other people by. You should be, like, a reporter or something."

Honesty looked really spooked. "You scare me sometimes, Vi. I get the feeling you can actually read my mind."

Whoops, I thought. "Hey, I get the odd psychic flash," I said aloud. "It's no biggie, honestly."

Honesty shook her head. "It's a bit more than a psychic flash, or you couldn't know my secret ambition." She took a breath. "Up until last spring, that's exactly what I wanted to be, this hotshot news reporter. You know the kind that report back from dangerous war zones?"

I was scared to breathe or change my expression.

Honesty's voice cracked. "Papa never took Rose's dreams seriously. It's one of the things I feel bad about. But he really encouraged me. We used to discuss the news when he got back from work, and he'd buy me these notebooks. I'd record all the things I saw and heard, sort of training myself for the day I could be a real reporter."

Keep talking, I prayed.

She swallowed. "I'd give anything to have those books back."

"Why? What happened to them?" I said casually, as if I hadn't watched her diaries turn into a heap of curly black ash.

"I burned them. I couldn't stand to look at

them, after he, erm, after he . . ."

Say it, I thought.

"After he . . . he . . . he died," she managed finally.

Whoosh!

I felt a surge of cosmic power go shimmering through our energy fields, as if for just a moment, Honesty Bloomfield and I were one.

She had done it! Honesty had somehow found the strength to disconnect herself from PODS FM. And I had this involuntary mental image of all the angel trainees on the GA hotline, clapping and cheering.

I could tell Honesty had no idea what had just happened. She just looked really spaced suddenly. I took her arm, and said gently, "Let's go home."

That night I heard a funny sound coming from her bed. I listened to her trying to muffle her huge racking sobs, then I went to sit beside her.

"It's okay," I said. "It's totally okay to cry when your dad dies. It's normal. Actually, it's necessary."

"You don't understand." She wept. "I'm not just crying because he's dead. I'm crying because I killed him."

"Don't be stupid," I said gently. "The poor guy was hit by a truck."

"You don't understand. I was a spoiled brat, Violet," she burst out. "I knew I was his favorite and I used it. I knew exactly how to twist him around my finger. Papa didn't want to get a car, but I kept on and on, like Chinese water torture, until he gave in. I killed him! I murdered my own papa and now I'll never see him again."

I ached to comfort her—but then I thought of Caleb Jones saying how people sometimes need to go into the dark and come out the other side. So I just sat with her quietly, until she cried herself to sleep.

And then I took my mobile out on to the balcony. I sat down in a calming yoga pose in the Californian darkness, and with pink, green, purple, and yellow advertising signs flashing all round me, I punched in the number of the GA hotline.

Honesty had remembered how to laugh and dance and have a good time. She'd started to grieve for her dead papa. She'd even remembered why she was here on Earth. In my opinion my work was done. I waited for Orlando to pick up. "Come on," I muttered.

"Mel, hi. How are you doing?" said a cool voice.

I was so horrified, I actually dropped my mobile.

I imagined it, I told myself frantically. I'm so paranoid about Brice being back in Heaven, I actually imagined I heard his voice.

I held the phone shakily to my ear. "Orlando?"

"I'm afraid lover boy's buzzed off on some secret mission, sweetheart," the voice said calmly. "You'll have to make do with me."

It was him. A fallen angel was manning the GA hotline. The entire cosmos had turned upside down!

Calm down, I scolded myself. You're okay with this, remember? Trees, diamonds, evolution, and whatever? Now act like a professional.

Unfortunately, when I'm shocked, my voice shoots up about two octaves. "Do you think you could ask the Agency to send me home?" I squeaked. "Honesty is pretty much sorted."

"You reckon?" Brice sounded so disbelieving that I wanted to smack him one.

"I'm telling you, she's back on track," I said sniffily.

"Oh yeah? And how long will that last if her

big brother screws up?"

I felt an unpleasant sinking feeling. "I don't get you."

"Sure you do," he said. "All those harmless little deliveries for the Top Hat's special customers. Those late night trips to the florists, hint, hint."

I found myself picturing the Lenny lookalike in the doorway. "Omigosh." I gasped. "That guy didn't just look like Lenny. He *was* Lenny!"

I had been so wrapped up in Honesty, I had totally failed to notice that the Franco brothers were dangerous gangsters!

"I am *so* dense!" I groaned.

To my astonishment, Brice said, "You're not dense, darling, you were just being focused. Luckily you're an angel, so you still absorbed the relevant info. Think back. What have Lenny's vibes been telling you?"

This is an exercise we do in class to develop our angelic intuition, but I have to say that doing it with Brice felt deeply disturbing.

"I think Lenny feels like everyone's doing much better than he is," I said slowly. "Ruby's doing her cabaret act and he has to wait on tables and see loud-mouthed customers throwing dollars around, like they're big somebodies. I think Lenny wanted to make some fast cash so he could be a big somebody too."

Then Brice said something really chilling.

"He forgot his dream," he said quietly. "And when humans forget why they're on Earth, the PODS are never far behind."

Chapter Ten

IT WAS THE WEEK BEFORE Christmas and fairy lights had gone up along Sunset Boulevard. But instead of beaming peace, goodwill, and whatever to humankind, I was in the depths of despair.

My mission was about to go pear-shaped. Lenny had stupidly got himself mixed up with rum-running racketeers. If I didn't find a way to help him, he'd probably get thrown in jail, Honesty would almost certainly go back into zombie mode, and the cosmic scoreboard would read PODS: two, Melanie Beeby: absolutely *nada*.

As I washed and dried endless glasses at the club, I racked my brains, trying to think of a solution. Maybe I should confront Lenny, tell him I knew what he was up to and advise him to clean up his act, before it was too late? That's definitely what the human part of me wanted to do. But my inner angel told me to wait and see just a little longer.

One night, Honesty and I were up in the projectionist's box at the Golden Picture Palace. Harold Lloyd was doing his mad stunts outside the top-floor window of a skyscraper, while Grace frantically kept up with the action on her plonky old piano. But neither of us were laughing that much, and I suddenly heard Honesty give a deep sigh.

"What's up?" I whispered, as Harold Lloyd almost, but not quite, plummeted to his doom.

"It's Mama," she whispered back. "She's worried she'll be out of a job now the talkies are coming in."

I'd heard customers talking about the new-style "talking pictures" in the Top Hat a few days ago. They were getting incredibly overexcited, as if movies with soundtracks were some mind-blowingly futuristic invention. I couldn't help wondering what they'd make of Dolby surround-sound! To me, the "talkies" (as Honesty called them) were totally inevitable. But like with all new scientific advances, there were going to be casualties. Once films had soundtracks of their own, the movie houses would no longer need pianists to provide dramatic mood music.

I broke my Reese's Peanut Butter Cup into two and gave Honesty half. I had become totally addicted to this rather weird American sweet. "Your mother is a born survivor," I said. "She'll find a job that pays heaps better, I bet you."

Honesty looked grateful. "You're always so positive, Violet. No matter how low I'm feeling you always make me feel better. I used to feel low all the time." She started saying all these really flattering things, but for some reason it was really hard to take it in. I seemed to be getting this weird disturbance in my energy field. *Omigosh, Lenny!* I thought, and I jumped to my feet.

Honesty stopped in mid-compliment. "Violet, what's wrong?"

"We've got to go to the club." I pulled Honesty to her feet. I knew I was spooking her again, but I didn't have a choice. "I've had one of my psychic flashes. Lenny's in danger!"

We were just a block away when I saw the prohibition agents. Okay, so I'd never seen a prohibition agent in my life, but I have watched no end of Sky TV, so a fleet of parked cars full of guys in raincoats and slouch hats naturally made me think the worst. Not to mention the humongous number of cops warily making their way toward the Top Hat.

"There's going to be a bust," I told Honesty.

"That's terrible." She gasped. "If the cops raid the club they'll put everyone in jail!"

We'd been working at the club for a while now, so we knew all its unofficial exits and entrances. Honesty and I dived down an alleyway, and managed to sneak in through the Top Hat's cellars without being seen. Ruby was just coming out of her dressing room. I could hear her muttering a prayer in Spanish, psyching herself up to do her act.

She looked startled. "What's up? I thought this was your night off?"

"You and Lenny have to get out of here!" I panted out. "There's, like, an army of cops and agents outside."

Ruby wasn't the kind of girl who needed things spelled out. "Quickly, we've got to find Lenny!"

We found him in the kitchens, lighting about a zillion sparklers on a customer's birthday cake. To my surprise, he totally didn't think of himself when we broke the news.

"This is terrible," he said anxiously. "Harold Lloyd just came in with his friends. We've got to get him out of here."

Lenny peered through the swing doors into the club and gave a moan of despair. "He's right down by the stage. It's jam-packed in there. The cops will be all over us like a rash, before I can get anywhere near him."

"But there's two of us!" Ruby reminded him softly.

She and Lenny exchanged glances.

"Are you thinking what I think you're thinking?" he asked.

She kissed her fingers to him, and without a word, they ran up the steps and burst through the swing door into the club.

Someone was in the middle of a raunchy dance routine to *Second Hand Rose*. Honesty and I arrived in time to hear all the musicians stop playing in a jangle of discordant notes.

The Top Hat Club had a high churchlike ceiling. A double row of chandeliers hung over the tables, their crystal drops trembling and tinkling with the tiniest vibration. With breathtaking confidence, Ruby and Lenny leaped onto a table and made a synchronized leap for the chandeliers. The customers gasped as Lenny and his sweetheart soared high over their heads, using the chandeliers for their trapeze!

"This is totally luminous!" I said to Honesty excitedly. "See what they're doing!"

Suspended from the Top Hat's ceiling was an enormous net, containing thousands of party balloons, which were due to come bobbing down at the end of the night's entertainment. As Lenny and Ruby swung crazily from one chandelier to another, they gradually pulled the net with them, in the process releasing brightly colored balloons, streamers, and glittery confetti over the astonished and delighted customers. Everyone began to clap and whistle, thinking it was all part of the show.

They reached a startled-looking Harold Lloyd. When they were performing, Lenny and Ruby were so in tune with each other that they read each other's minds. Without exchanging even a glance, they both hooked a foot around a chandelier and flipped upside down. And still dangling like a bat, Lenny whispered in Harold Lloyd's ear.

I saw the star's expression change as he took

in the news. He nodded. Lenny and Ruby held out the net with a flourish, and the star sprang into the air and clung to the meshes for dear life.

Honesty's brother and his feisty girlfriend swung Harold Lloyd back across the club at electrifying speed. The trio did a graceful dismount, waved cheekily to the customers, and made a lightning getaway through the swing doors and out of the back of the club.

We caught up with Lenny and Ruby, just as Harold Lloyd dived into a cab and went screeching off in the totally opposite direction of the advancing law enforcement agents. I couldn't believe what had just happened. I had come *this* close to meeting a world-famous movie star!

Lenny was staring at a card with an incredulous expression.

"Was he grateful?" Honesty asked.

"Oh, yeah," said Lenny in a stunned voice. "Yeah, he was."

"He was only drinking root beer," said Ruby dreamily. "But it would have looked really bad for the studios if one of their big stars was involved with a bust."

"So what did he say to you?" Honesty asked eagerly.

Lenny still seemed overwhelmed. "He said, erm . . ." He cleared his throat. "He said we were the hottest stunt duo he had ever seen, and he told us to call him at the studios tomorrow."

"Omigosh, he *didn't*!" I screamed. "That is *so* fabulous, Lenny!"

"Just as well," Ruby said calmly. "After tonight, it looks like we'll be needing new jobs."

I saw that the Top Hat Club was now totally surrounded by law enforcement agents. Violent battering sounds came from the front of the building. A cop was bellowing through a megaphone, ordering everyone to come out with their hands in the air.

I put my mouth to Honesty's ear. "Do you think Mo and Izzy are in that crowd somewhere, in a couple of cheesy disguises?" I said wickedly.

At the same moment we bleated, "Dere's saaad news!"

And we all linked arms and walked away from the mayhem, still laughing.

It was Christmas Eve, and I was helping Honesty stow the last of her luggage in the back of a rented car. Honesty, Rose, Clem, and their mother were finally traveling on to San Francisco, where Grace was going to run a boutique for her scandalous cousin Louella. I'd got Honesty to give me the juicy details by this time, so I can tell you that by the standards of my century, Louella was disappointingly tame. Know what her big crime was? She had the nerve to marry a really dishy Chinese guy! I'm serious! Unfortunately in the American south of the Twenties, this was enough to give her a reputation as a serious scarlet woman. But something told me she was going to be an excellent friend for Grace.

Rose was going to find work in San Francisco until what I called the autumn, and she called the fall. Can you guess what little Miss Smarty Pants was going to do then? Yess! She was actually starting college, just as she'd always dreamed. Like Michael said, things work out.

Honesty squished in the last bag and shut what she called the trunk and I called the boot.

"And you'll really be all right?" she asked me for the tenth time.

"I told you, I'll be fine," I said softly.

She shifted her feet, suddenly shy. "I don't know if I'll ever get used to Christmas in Los

Angeles. Don't you think it feels unnatural, Violet? I mean, sleighs and Santas, when the temperature is in the nineties?"

I smiled to myself. I had a different take on Christmas. I knew that this City of the Angels was Christmassy in every way that mattered. I could feel every sleazy glitzy inch of LA shimmering and tingling with joyful cosmic vibes, like peals of bells only I could hear. "I almost forgot," I said. "I've got something for you."

I handed Honesty the Christmas present I had bought for her with my wages from the Top Hat. "Go on, open it!"

She unwrapped the layers of tissue paper and gasped. "Ohh, Violet! It's the most beautiful notebook I've ever seen."

"Yeah, well use it, Bloomfield," I told her. "Stick everything down. All the hobos, hoodlums, and holy rollers. The bootleggers, rum-runners, and speakeasies. The whole shebang."

The shimmery Christmas vibes were growing so intense that that it was overwhelming, even for an angel. I saw Honesty's eyes fill with awe. She almost seemed scared. "Who are you, really, Violet?" she whispered.

I kissed her on the cheek. "I'm your friend,

nutcase. Any time you need me, just call, okay?"

A beam of heavenly light strobed down, and as Honesty watched, dazzled and amazed, I stepped into it and went home.

Chapter Eleven

A FEW DAYS AFTER I GOT BACK from my GA mission, I dragged my soul mate along to the school library.

"I want to see if I can find any mention of a hotshot news reporter called Honesty Bloomfield," I explained. "I want to know if things turned out okay for her."

Lollie just looked at me with her knowing brown eyes, and I sighed and owned up.

"I suppose, what I really want to know is if I made the grade as a guardian angel."

She gave me a hug. "You don't have to justify yourself to me, Boo," she said. "Being a guardian angel is pretty intense. You can't switch off and stop caring just because your assignment is over. You need closure."

"Hey, that's right!" I said.

I needed to know that I'd made a difference to

Honesty Bloomfield. After her dad died, her life was like this scary and depressing movie, one that was scripted and directed by the PODS. With the Agency's help, she'd found the courage to break free. But I wanted to know what happened next. Did Honesty get to direct her own life movie? Did she finally become the kind of person who called the shots?

Lollie and I went on with our search. Can you believe that we found about a zillion mentions? We could see that we were in for a long session, so we got comfortable on the floor between the stacks, and updated ourselves.

Lola gave a low whistle. "Boy, Melanie! Your girl really got around!"

She wasn't exaggerating. Honesty went everywhere. She was over in Europe covering some of the major events in the Second World War. She also went to Singapore and Cairo and sent back some brilliant reports.

It was Lola who found the photographs, black and white and slightly out of focus. In one a taller, skinnier Honesty was posing in front of the Pyramids. She wore her long hair in that brushed-back Thirties style. I thought she looked amazingly elegant in her army camouflage gear, screwing up her eyes against the sun.

In another picture, Honesty was at an old-fashioned typewriter. Tropical sunshine streamed through a slatted window. She wore her camouflage shirt open at the neck and her sleeves rolled up. She wasn't doing one of those cheesy celebrity smiles, just looking coolly back at the camera, with that interested gleam in her eye. Honesty had made it.

By this time I was on a roll, so I went into the film history section to see what the movies buffs had to say about Tony Mantovani's movies. To my disappointment, I drew a complete blank.

"I don't get it," I said to myself.

"Hi, Mel. How's it going?" Brice came mooching round the stacks, looking distinctly dangerous in a way you totally don't expect in an angelic library.

I decided to play it cool.

"I'm trying to find Tony Mantovani," I said carelessly. "He made a movie called *Dangerous Pearls*, and Honesty's sister played the heroine, but no one seems to have heard of it."

"Did you check through their old movie collection?" he suggested.

I didn't tell him I hadn't known our library

possessed an old movie collection. I just rushed off to ask the librarian, and a few minutes later she pushed a heavy metal spool across the counter. "Director's cut," she said proudly.

My mouth fell open. "This is the actual film!"

"The original copy of *Dangerous Pearls* was destroyed in a warehouse fire, not long after it was finished," said the librarian. "But as you know, we keep copies of every film ever made."

"Omigosh!" I shrieked.

Several angel trainees looked up from their books and said, "Sssh!"

I wandered around until I found Brice. "But how will I watch it?" I said pathetically. "It's, like, really old technology."

He gave a deep sigh and took me to a door near the library's spiral staircase. I peered wonderingly into a dinky retro movie theater, which I had completely never noticed. It had plushy seats, red velvet curtains, a screen, and best of all, an old-fashioned movie projector.

"Have fun, sweetheart," said Brice and he mooched off again, doing his dangerous bad-boy walk. As he went, I thought, well that wasn't *so* bad, Melanie. Providing you only meet him in totally public places.

That night I took all my mates to the movies. We did it American style, with popcorn and Hershey's Kisses and Reese's Peanut Butter Cups.

Chase started up the projector, and I heard it starting to whirr in the dark. I hugged myself happily. It was almost as good as being in the Golden Palace Picture House. The film had been remastered to re-create the full Twenties film experience. As the title *Dangerous Pearls* came up, humongously dramatic piano music filled the theater. I know, I know, I should have acted really cool and laid-back and let my mates watch the film in peace, but I just couldn't help interrupting. I kept going, "Oh, that's Clem with the puppy. Mr. Mantovani hated that poor animal. It kept widdling on his shoes," and, "Rose could have been a famous celebrity, you know, but she wanted to be an intellectual, so what can you do?" I was so proud that I had actually been with them while this film was being made.

"Oh, you've got to watch this bit," I said suddenly. "This is where they tied poor Rose to the train tracks. Honesty was convinced she was going to be mashed by an express train. I wasn't too happy either, so I surrounded Rose with—*Omigosh!*"

Lola laughed. "Hey, Boo, you're a celebrity!"

I gazed in pure astonishment at the screen.

The scene was very nearly as I remembered it, with Rose miming wide-eyed terror, and the villain pulling evil expressions.

But now three people were in the shot: the heroine, the villain, and a girl in a pink Kung Fu Kitty T-shirt and boot-cut jeans.

"But how . . . ?" I breathed. "I wasn't even visible, not then."

"This is the heavenly copy," Reuben said softly.

"But I look—I look . . ."

I was so happy, I'd lost the power of speech.

Like an angel, I thought. I look exactly like an angel.

ANGELS UNLIMITED

Read all of Mel's exciting adventures!

1 Winging It

Mel isn't your average angel. Not in her wildest dreams did she expect to wind up at the posh Angel Academy. Who would want to learn about halos, when shopping is so much more divine? But when Mel joins an elite group of time-traveling angels fighting against the Opposition, she learns angel business is a lot more dangerous and a whole lot more fun than she ever imagined.

2 Losing the Plot

Mel and her two best mates have been given an exclusive assignment—to rescue a troublesome teenage trio in sixteenth-century London. But what's so special about these three? When disaster strikes their mission, Mel has to act *fast*.

3 Flying High

After all that time-traveling, all Mel wants to do is relax and go to her pal Lola's surprise party. It's so unfair when she and her friends get sent off to medieval times at the last minute. When she gets there, she discovers a seriously dangerous scam that has got to be fixed.

4 Calling the Shots

If there's any place a teenage angel wants to go, it has got to be Hollywood. So when Mel gets sent on her first solo assignment to America in the 1920s, she's super excited. But things are a lot more dangerous in tinseltown than she expected. Can Mel make it on her own?